BABSON, MARIAN

DEATH BESIDE THE SEA.

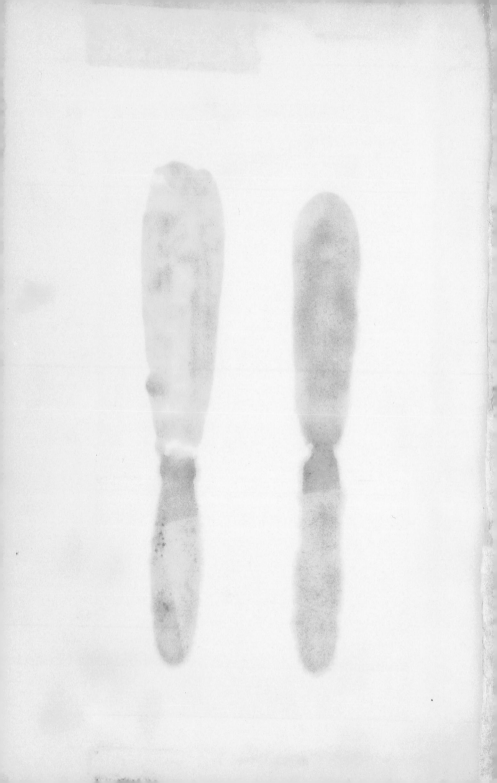

Death Beside the Sea

Death Beside the Sea

MARIAN BABSON

WALKER AND COMPANY
NEW YORK

First published in the United States of America in 1983 by the Walker Publishing Company, Inc.

ISBN: 0-8027-5490-2

Library of Congress Catalog Card Number: 82-51309

Printed in the United States of America

10 9 8 7 6 5 4 3 2 1

CHAPTER 1

He was a Saturday-night Starer.

I can't help it, they frighten me. There's no way you can reach them. You can smile sweetly at them, send them a chummy wink, offer them a request number—but it doesn't work. They won't meet your eyes, they won't give any sign that they recognize you as a human being, or even that they're human themselves. If you persist, they slide away, dissolving into the shadows they sprang from.

Then, just when you're beginning to relax again, you suddenly feel those eyes boring into you from some far corner of the room and you don't have to turn around to know that your Starer's back. Staring.

They're always in the far corner of the room, always in the shadows, always alone. Naturally. They're born loners, the Starers. If they could make any kind of contact with another human being, they wouldn't be lurking in a corner, nursing their drink and staring, would they?

I pressed down on the loud pedal, beamed my brightest smile towards that corner, and said cheerily, 'All right now, it's time for special requests. Who'd like to hear a favourite song? How about that handsome gentleman over in the . . . ?'

He was gone. Drifted away like smoke in the way they always do. So insubstantial that, after a few moments, you couldn't swear that they'd been there at all. As for ever describing one of them, forget it. How do you describe a swirl of smoke in a smoky room? He was a Saturday-night Starer, that's all. You run into them every now and again. Sometimes, like tonight, they show up on other nights of the week, as well. They're an occupational hazard. I just hadn't expected to run into one over here, that's why he jarred me so. Silly of me. It's the same all over the world, we all know that. Or we would, if we let ourselves think about it at any length.

The less inhibited were shouting out their requests now and I let my fingers rove over the keyboard plinking out encouraging chords. They were the more usual weekend audience: friendly, relaxed, out for a good time. Easy to please, willing to meet you half way to be entertained. So nice, so normal.

I brightened my smile to disguise the fact that I'd never heard of half the numbers they were calling for. I was still fairly new here. But I'd learn, I'd learn . . .

The room hushed abruptly and I realized that I'd unconsciously slipped into Rimsky-Korsakov: *Scheherazade*. Probably the effect the Starer had on me. My subconscious identified with the frightened girl keeping death at bay by the flimsy power of her ability to keep a capricious tyrant entertained . . . entranced.

How Freudian can you get?

My fingers faltered and stumbled as I tried to segue into something more suitable for a cocktail-bar audience on a Bank Holiday Friday night. But they wouldn't let me.

'Keep going, lass,' a voice roared out. There was a spattering of applause. Incredibly, they were enjoying it. They didn't want anything I might consider more suitable. They wanted *Scheherazade*.

I went along with it for a while, the music soothing me as much as them. As I came towards the end of the movement, I leaned forward into the microphone.

'You know,' I said chummily, 'you may not believe it, but there are lyrics to this. No, honestly,' I answered the ripple of laughter. 'We used it for a Television Spectacular once. Oh yes, I can just hear you saying, "Those Americans would do anything . . ." '

It got another laugh. But suddenly, I wished I hadn't said it.

He was back. I could feel those eyes boring into me. Without looking up, I knew which corner he was in. Staring . . . and listening . . . and staring . . .

Staring with those ice-cold impersonal eyes. What was going on behind them?

God knows what they imagine themselves doing with you. Or to you. But, whatever it is, it's a pretty safe bet that you're not going to enjoy it.

But that doesn't matter. Because you're not human. You're the cut-out doll from the centre-page spread, the plastic body without any feelings, the inflatable rubber doll from the sex shop. He's the only one in all the world who can feel anything—and you wouldn't want to know what he's feeling.

It was time for another vocal, but I didn't think my voice would stand up to it. Even my fingers stumbled over the intro. I flashed a smile and started again.

'It's all right, Trudi.' Ted was beside me, setting a glass of chilled white wine on top of the piano for me. 'I've spotted him. I'll go over and tell him to hop it. We don't want his sort around here.'

Ted moved off purposefully and I half-turned on the piano bench to follow his progress. But the Starer was gone again. There was just an empty seat in the corner from which I had felt those eyes boring into me.

It was unlikely that he'd be back tonight. Not now that he knew Ted would be watching out for him.

But would he be waiting outside when I left for the night?

'*Bless Them All!*' Someone called out the title and, since it was a number I knew, I swung into it. Voices joined in from all over the room. There was laughter and the bustle of waitresses serving fresh drinks. Everything was the way it ought to be again. Inside here.

'Sorry about that.' Ted was back. 'He got away, but he won't get in here again. I'll see to that.' He hesitated. 'I'll see you home tonight, too.'

'Thanks.' I turned off the mike and pressed down on the loud pedal while I kept playing to cover our conversation. 'I'd appreciate that. I . . . I feel a bit silly, but he really spooked me.'

'Nothing silly about it,' Ted said. 'You can't be too careful this weekend. There's a lot of riff-raff about.' He ran a gloomy eye over his customers, most of whom, although spending money like drunken sailors, failed to find favour with him.

'You've heard our expression, "Where's there's muck, there's brass," ' he said. 'Well, you can turn it round the other way and still be right: "Where there's brass, there's muck." ' Again he surveyed his customers with distaste. 'Muck!'

I looked around the room myself with what was becoming an increasingly expert eye. They weren't that bad. They weren't the regulars, of course. Not tonight. This was the Friday-night start of the long August Bank Holiday weekend. The regulars would all be keeping their own places open, tending to their own hordes of tourists down spending money on the last big holiday of the year until Christmas. Something else that was the same all over the world.

There were a few of the two-week holidaymakers, winding up their yearly holiday this weekend. The rest were strangers, people down from London for the long weekend; perhaps some of them starting their own two-week holiday a bit late in the year. All perfectly respectable people, so far as I could tell.

But Ted was viewing them all with a jaundiced eye. In fact, the whole town was. Everyone feared a recurrence of the events of last August Bank Holiday, when marauding gangs of motor-cyclists had invaded the seaside resort, fought among themselves, vandalized the shops and terrorized the townspeople until, finally, they receded like the tide. Like the tide, leaving bits of flotsam and jetsam to mark their passage: empty beer cans, splintered shop-front windows, a few of their number marooned in hospital with knife wounds and broken bones, and the naked body of a young girl lying on the beach just by the Grand Pier.

She had never been identified. Only last week, the local newspaper had run a series of follow-up articles on the events of that Bank Holiday weekend, pointing out — unnecessarily — that such things must never be allowed to happen again in Our Fair City. The final article had dwelt sadly on the idea that such a young girl — surely someone's daughter, sister, cousin, friend — could disappear from what must be her accustomed haunts and never be missed.

No one had been able to identify her from the published photograph and the police had come to the conclusion that she had come down to the seaside with the motor-cycle gangs, probably as a pillion passenger, and been abandoned either when her dead body had been discovered (but not reported) by the gang, or when she had failed to turn up at their rendezvous for the return trip to town.

There had been further speculation that she might be a foreigner, some little *au pair* who had perhaps quarrelled with the family where she was supposed to be living and had taken herself off with some exciting boy-friend. Her erstwhile employers would assume that she had returned to her native country; her family would assume that she was still living happily in England and learning to speak the language like a native, although not a good correspondent in any language. Either way, it could be several more months — or years — before anyone thought to institute the enquiries that would eventually lead to the discovery of her fate.

I was glad I hadn't been here at the time. My piano bar was situated at the long floor-to-ceiling window overlooking the Grand Pier with a fine view of the beach — if I turned round. There were moments when it was disturbing enough just thinking about what had happened without actually having been here to see it then. No wonder the town was tense tonight, with people jumping at the sound of a car backfiring. I'd jump myself at anything I thought was a motor-cycle and I'd only experienced the whole thing second-hand, through the newspaper articles and the stories and remarks of the people who'd lived through it.

Ted was still glowering around the crowded room, looking out for trouble. He'd even have welcomed a return of the Starer, I suspected. It would give him some-one to challenge. He didn't like a waiting role and that was all any of us had right now. Waiting for trouble we hoped wasn't going to come. There was no reason why it should.

The police were waiting, too, and the gangs knew it. They had descended on other seaside towns during this long, if not hot, summer. Always a different town, always over a weekend—but there was no record of their having gone back to a place a second time. Not that that signified anything. The very unpredictability of their manic forays meant that nothing could be foreseen about their be-haviour. Weeks would go by peacefully and then some quiet resort would be descended on and devastated before the police could call in enough reserves to get the situation under control.

It wasn't a new phenomenon. It appeared to have oc-curred periodically over the past twenty-five years or so, but it always took the authorities by surprise because it skipped generations. Just as they thought the rivalries and gang warfare had died out, suddenly there were new gangs, new rivalries and new raids on unsuspecting towns, arbi-trarily chosen as battlefields, well away from their own territories. In the beginning, they had made their way to the battlegrounds by train and bus, now the standard of living had risen and they had their own motor-cycles, thus

expediting their getaways and making it harder to catch
them.

'Right . . .' Ted said, in reluctant admission that things
were probably as peaceful as they seemed. He turned and
looked through the big plate glass window behind me,
checking the beach, the Grand Pier, the trippers promen-
ading along the sea front. I turned and caught him
staring out to sea.

'*I saw the harbour lights* . . .' The song seemed to ripple
from my fingers and throat of its own accord and I continued with it. It was gently nostalgic, sad and haunting,
but peaceful. I stole another glance at Ted and saw a smile
tugging at the corner of his mouth. It was soothing him,
as I had intended it to. The customers seemed to be
enjoying it, as well. But they were an undemanding bunch,
on holiday, they'd have enjoyed anything.

Then Ted glanced down and the smile was wiped away. I
knew that he was looking at the foreshore, where the body
had lain. Right across from his pub.

It was a posher pub now, trying hard to be a high-class
cocktail-bar with entertainment along American lines — a
new departure for the English seaside, I gathered. Ted
called it The Phoenix because it had risen from the flames
and wreckage of the old pub. The insurance had paid for
most of it and a fresh infusion of money from a new
partner had taken care of the rest.

'Tomorrow, they'll likely start coming.' Ted turned
back to me. 'Or Sunday, that's when they can raise the
most hell. Because some of them have to work on Sat-
urdays, but they've got Sunday and Monday clear. Sunday . . . that's when they came before.'

He rubbed his left arm thoughtfully, the arm that had
been broken that night.

The crowd was thinning out now, it was close to closing
time. There was no one left sitting around the piano, not
that there had been many earlier. The regulars weren't

here tonight and the arrangement always came as a shock to new people who had never seen such a thing before. By tomorrow, they'd be used to the idea and I could count on a full house. Right now, I could talk freely, so long as I kept playing and leaned away from the mike.

'They won't come back,' I said. 'They never do.'

'They might.' He flexed his fingers. 'And this time, I'll be ready.'

They could never do so much damage again, in any case. The Phoenix was on the first floor. Ted would never operate anything at ground level again. You can't ride a motor-cycle up a flight of stairs.

The ground floor had been taken over by the local Chamber of Commerce as a Tourist Office. It was open from 9 a.m. to 6 p.m. and sold maps, postcards, tickets to the shows playing on the Grand Pier and at the other theatres around town. They also offered bus tours to the local attractions: The Stately Home with the Safari Park in the grounds (combination ticket available); the local Freak of Nature; the surrounding Beauty Spots (picnic lunch included); and the side trips to neighbouring towns and shopping centres. They also gave advice, provided lists of Bed and Breakfast accommodation, arranged rail travel and acted as agents for the day trips to France running from the neighbouring port.

The Tourist Office's chief virtue in Ted's eyes was the hours it kept. Open during the day and closed at night, it provided no competition and offered no distraction. To the contrary, trippers visiting it during the day would often take advantage of the proximity of The Phoenix to nip upstairs for a quick one before catching their bus or going out on the Grand Pier; while, dark and shuttered at night, it presented no temptation to the most determined tearaway to smash his way inside and start trying to vandalize a rack of travel brochures.

Ted had always firmly denied the occasional accusation

that the fact that his brother-in-law, Albert Tiverton, was a Councillor had had anything to do with his having rented the ground-floor accommodation so fortuitously. Thousands wouldn't have believed him—including many of the townspeople—but I did. I knew his brother-in-law.

Oh, not well. No better than you would wish to know a beefy, beery man who pinched your behind upon introduction and made ponderous *double entendres* about the Special Relationship. Only one thing could be said in his favour: he wasn't a Starer. His eyes just plain lit up and read 'Tilt!'

It had taken some fast and fancy footwork over the next few weeks, but I thought that Councillor Tiverton was finally getting the message. He hadn't dropped in for some time now.

Of course, it was the height of the Season and he had his own interests. Foremost among them was an amusement arcade called (wouldn't you know it?) The Fun Palace, which bestrode the entrance to the Grand Pier. You couldn't get out on the pier without passing through it. It was a combination penny arcade and hall of mirrors with a joke shop specializing in whoopee cushions, fur spiders and plastic dog dirt tucked away in one corner. It was very popular with the visiting children and the more immature specimens among their parents.

I had met his wife, Milly, Ted's sister, even more rarely. She seemed a docile, downtrodden, rather discouraged woman who would have profited by having been introduced to Women's Lib at an early age. Or, even now, being introduced to a sharp double-bladed axe with the firm assurance that no jury on earth would convict her.

'Right, that's it,' Ted said, as a few more stragglers got up and headed for the exit. He raised his voice. 'Time, gentlemen, please!'

'*Good night, Ladies*' . . . I began playing as the lights dipped. I had learned that song beat even the calling of

'Time' as a notice of dismissal from which there was no appeal.

Glasses were emptied hastily, goodbyes called out, the room began emptying. I kept playing until the last of them had gone and then I turned to look out of the window.

The lights on the Grand Pier had dimmed for the night. The moon had disappeared behind a cloud. It seemed later and colder than it really was. The crowd along the promenade had thinned; those who remained no longer seemed so cheerful and innocent.

It reminded me that there was a Starer somewhere out there. Perhaps staring at the last of the customers drifting out of The Phoenix . . . waiting . . .

'Get your coat, Trudi,' Ted said. 'I'm seeing you home tonight. Aye, and the rest of the weekend, as well. You'll be all right with me.'

CHAPTER 2

The town rose up from the sea front in tiers, like a wedding-cake. At sea level, there was the Lower Town, a flat basin stretching back for half a mile, heavily built up with hotels along the sea front, fish and chip shops, fancy restaurants, catchpenny stalls and places of amusement featuring every possible permutation of dream, fantasy or nightmare which might be reckoned to extract a few more pence from the pockets of indiscriminate tourists. It had taken me a while to get used to it. I think they call it culture shock.

Even the sea itself looked alien to my eyes. Accustomed as I was to the open sea and sky and rolling sand dunes of Long Island and Cape Cod, the English seacoast looked miniature and claustrophobic, enervated and overcontrolled, subdued—not to say, beaten into submission.

Instead of a wide unbroken stretch of sand, this was a mile-long stretch of shale, lightly powdered with imported sand, bounded at one end by the Grand Pier, a Victorian extravaganza extending an endless length straight out to sea, with more shops and stalls along its length and the Grand Theatre marking the end of it. At the other end of the beach was the Minor Pier, smaller in every way, decommissioned now and totally given over to the Yacht Club belonging to the Marina on the far side of the Minor Pier. The Marina was a new development. An artificial harbour had been dredged out, a sea wall erected around it and, ashore, a number of blocks of flats had been ranged along the front and were already changing hands at prices way beyond the original purchase price. Already, too, small new shops were clustering around the original grocery store and ships' chandlers. In time, the area would undoubtedly become known as the New Town, and the Upper and Lower Town be relegated to the status of Old Town.

The first tier of the Lower Town was given over to lodging-houses, antique shops, more restaurants, and shops for the practical necessities of life, like chemists, shoe repairers and newsagents/tobacconists. There was also the inevitable proliferation of charity second-hand shops. On a wet day, the sea front was deserted while the trippers browsed for hours through the cast-off delights offered in the side streets and winding passageways of the first tier.

The second tier was the point at which the Lower Town and Upper Town met, although no one ever referred to it by anything so Transatlantic sounding as Mid-Town. This was where the foresighted Founding Fathers had placed the Town Hall and various public amenities, such as the library and sports field, high enough above sea level to be beyond the reach of a flood tide. This was also where you found the Sainsbury's, the Woolworth's, the Marks and Spencer's, and those other ubiquitous chain stores which dominated every High Street across the land.

The third and fourth tiers were residential, where the people of the town actually lived, retreating up there after they had spent a busy day earning money down on the sea front. The schools, both of them, were tucked away here, too.

The final tier was the great plateau that levelled off and rolled back across green acres to become part of the agricultural inland, linking up eventually with the motorway leading to London.

At the top of this plateau, looking out over town and sea, huddled the nursing homes and sanatoria, strategically placed by their Victorian builders to allow invalids the benefits of the sea breezes, while discouraging all but the hardiest and nearest-mended from descending to the town and dissipating their feeble energies on the frivolous amusements it offered. Tradition dies hard and the nursing homes and sanatoria endured to this day, sheltering the elderly, the convalescent, those recovering from operations and, in at least one sanatorium, the mentally disordered.

Which reminded me of the Starer again. Had he come from up there? I shuddered.

'Bloody weather,' Ted grumbled. 'I'll turn on the heater.' He leaned forward and did so. 'End of August and you couldn't tell the difference from bleedin' February. Except it was warmer in February.'

'Thanks,' I said gratefully. There was no point in trying to explain. Besides, it *was* cold. Not that it discouraged the holiday throngs. They seemed to just throw on another sweater and continue what passed for merrymaking with them. 'At least it isn't actually raining.'

'Better if it was,' Ted grunted. 'Bit of rain and the wrong sort might stay at home. Seaside's not much fun in the wet. Wouldn't hurt business, either. Those already here would just take their pleasures inside. Plenty to do in the arcades and shops and pubs.'

'More than enough to do indoors,' I agreed. There had better be, if this was a typical English summer.

The car laboured up a final hill, turned and drew to a stop. I was home—or what was passing for home these days. It would have been too expensive to stay in one of the hotels and too depressing to stay at one of the boarding-houses on the lower level. Fortunately, Ted had arranged for me to stay in what he called 'theatrical digs' in a house on the third tier, just comfortably above the noise and crowds of the Lower Town.

'Don't get out,' I said, as he began to move. 'I'll be all right now.'

'Ah well.' He settled back, rubbing the arm that had been broken. 'I'll wait and see you safe to the door. I don't like all those bushes there by the gate. Bloody daft place to have them, if you ask me. I'd cut them all down if they were mine.'

'Oh, but lilacs are so beautiful in the spring,' I said un-convincingly. Spring was long past, the scented purple blossoms had faded and gone, leaving dark clumps of shadowed rustling leaves behind which anything might be lurking. I shuddered again.

'Get inside,' Ted said. 'There's a mortal chill in the air tonight. And don't worry about anything. I'll make sure we don't have that one hanging about again.'

'Thanks.' I smiled feebly as I got out and slammed the car door behind me. I went up the path, not looking left nor right, but glad I had Ted waiting behind me, keeping watch.

The hall light was glowing and I was uneasily aware that I was silhouetted—a perfect target—as I turned to wave reassuringly to Ted from the doorway. I had shut the door and locked it behind me before I heard the car motor starting up again.

*

The Prime Minister of Mirth was sitting on the finial of the stair rail as I turned. He yawned a greeting, tail twitching.

'Good evening, George,' I said.

I got a double answer. Robey snorted, twitching his whiskers this time, and Formby appeared from nowhere to curl around my ankles, chirruping.

'All right, all right,' I said. 'Wait a minute, can't you?' I hunted for the plastic bag of leftovers which had slipped, as usual, to the bottom of my handbag. 'Where's Gracie?'

There was another answering chirrup and a marmalade shadow slid into the hallway from the dining-room, followed by another, altogether bulkier, figure.

'You spoil them, you do,' Daisy Dayton said in the gratified tones of a pet-lover who quite understands that her darlings are irresistible. 'Spoil them rotten.'

I found the bag of leftovers and brought it out. With a yowl of approval, Robey leaped to the floor, stretched, and led the procession to the kitchen.

'Slim pickings tonight, kids,' I shook the bite-sized pieces of cocktail sausages and cheese into the three bowls, trying for an equal division. 'The customers were hungry.'

'Trying to save themselves the cost of buying a meal later, more likely,' my landlady sniffed. 'You don't get the best sort on Bank Holiday weekends. I'm surprised Ted put out the good bits tonight. Peanuts and crisps are good enough for *them*.'

'It wasn't a bad audience,' I defended. 'Except for—'

That pair of burning eyes surfaced in my memory, cutting me off. I couldn't say what colour they were, nor could I bring into focus the nebulous white blur of a face surrounding them. He might pass me in the street tomorrow and I would not realize it—not so long as he kept his eyes lowered. But if he were to raise his head and look into my face—

I shuddered again.

'One of those, eh?' Daisy Dayton had been in The Profession herself, touring the Provinces in a dance troupe coyly called The Daisy Chain between the Wars and then as a member of ENSA ('Every Night, Something Awful, that's what they used to say,' she had confided cheerfully) during the war. She had had her share of experiences, good and bad, before the late Mr Dayton had detached her from The Daisy Chain and they had retired to the seaside. She had not lost contact with her former colleagues, however, and from putting up a few chums when they appeared at local theatres, she had passed almost imperceptibly through the stage of putting up friends of friends until she found herself a fully-fledged theatrical landlady whose 'digs' were prized as one of the better billets on the circuit.

'You mustn't let it get you down, dear,' she said. 'There are always some of those about.'

'I know,' I said. 'I guess I just wasn't expecting it here, that's all. It got to me.' I shuddered again and added apologetically, 'There've been some nasty cases in the States . . .'

'The world isn't what it used to be, dear.' She sighed. 'Things are getting nastier everywhere.'

Fields, too, was of this opinion. Formby, having gulped down the contents of his own dish, had sidled round to hers and helped himself to a piece of sausage. Fields laid back her ears and smacked him across the chops. Formby clenched his teeth in his prize and backed out of range. Fields crouched over her dish, her high-pitched growl rising threateningly.

'Sing it, Gracie,' Daisy cheered, diverted. 'Oh, you should have heard her in the old days!'

'Really?' I was momentarily startled. Fields could not be much more than three or four years old. And she sounded in fine voice to me.

'The *real* Gracie, I mean. Sorry, dear.' Daisy sighed again. 'I get carried away. I know they're not really their namesakes, really I do. But I like to pretend sometimes. It's why I named them the way I did, to begin with. Because I couldn't stand to think of people like that being gone from the world. This way, it seems as though they're still with us, almost. You don't mind, do you, dear?'

'Of course not,' I said. 'Why should I?' It was a fairly mild eccentricity, compared to some I had seen. If she could extract a degree of comfort from it, who was I to object?

'That's all right, then,' she said. 'Some people don't like it, you know. They say it gives them the creeps. As long as you don't mind—?' She paused delicately.

'I don't,' I affirmed. I had just had an encounter with something that genuinely produced the creeps. Innocent little Robey, Formby and Fields weren't even in the running with that.

'I didn't think you would.' She was obscurely satisfied. 'You're not that sort.'

Robey sat back on his haunches and looked from his empty dish to his two companions. Fields was the only one still eating and she gave another warning growl. Formby had begun circling her plate warily again. Robey decided it was all beneath him and settled back to wash his face majestically.

'Am I the last one in?'

'That's right, dear. I'll lock up for the night now. No one wants to be out late at a time like this. You never know . . .'

Ye shall know not the day nor the hour. It was not a comforting thought. It was not intended to be. But, for all the dark Testament echoes, she was right. No one was going to linger on the slopes of Town late at night this weekend.

Not unless they were tourists and didn't know any

better. But the occupants of this house had been here long enough to share in the general paranoia of the townspeople. They were going to lock the doors, batten down the hatches and keep the lowest of profiles until the danger of marauding invaders was over. I supposed it must have been like this in early times when Viking raiders were a constant threat to those living along the coastline. Vikings had receded into historical perspective and now the new danger came from within; from the young and bored who found their amusement in preying upon their own country.

'The Great Dandini came in just before you did, dear.' Daisy Dayton shot home the bolts with decisive clicks. 'I'd thought he might stay out a bit later, being a man and all, but he takes good care of himself.' She sniffed. 'Wants to live to be a great big star with his own show. But he'd better put in more rehearsal time. His act is getting slack, dear, very slack. He might think it doesn't matter, out there on the end of the pier, but the Public notices these things, dear. Even if they applaud just to be polite.'

'It's the end of the season, nearly.' I felt obscurely moved to defend the little man in the basement bedsitter. 'He's probably tired and gone a little stale.'

There were times enough when I found my own audiences exhausting. A sensitive performer doing three shows a day, trying to satisfy an audience of both adults and children must be close to the breakdown point by the end of summer. His audience-participation segment alone — with a myriad grubby little helpers trooping onstage to rap on the walls of his magic cabinet, look up his sleeves to assure themselves he concealed nothing but his arms, pull strings which turned into endless streamers of flags, and all the rest of the participation stunts — would have driven me out of my mind if I had to do it. However, the Great Dandini was an expert at coping with awkward little customers bent on either showing off or exposing the mechanics of his tricks. But just keeping that smile on his face at such times must have taken its toll.

'Of course, Norma and Little Johnny went up to bed ages ago.' Daisy continued counting her chickens. 'They must be well into the Land of Nod by now. Poor things.'

I nodded without comment. Certainly, Norma Handel would be asleep. She seemed to spend an inordinate amount of time sleeping. As to what Little Johnny might be doing while his mother slept, I wouldn't like to speculate. On at least three occasions, I was fairly sure I had spotted him flitting along the promenade at an hour when everyone would have thought him fast asleep. I'd never mentioned it, of course. Why add to Norma's troubles? If she didn't already suspect it, she'd find out soon enough that her son was uncontrollable. He wasn't particularly likeable, either. There was something sly about his eyes. I had also noticed that none of the cats remained in a room once he had entered it.

'There now!' Daisy splashed milk into each of the three bowls on the floor. It seemed to remind her of something. 'Are you sure you wouldn't like a little something yourself before you go upstairs, dear?'

'Quite sure, thanks,' I said. 'I'm just very tired. I think I'll go straight to bed.'

'You do that, dear. It doesn't pay to get overtired. An *artiste* lives on her nerves. Oh, *I* know . . .'

I smiled and slid away, escaping whatever reminiscences might be in the offing. Usually these glimpses of a lost world fascinated me, but tonight I was genuinely exhausted. I could feel the ache between my shoulder-blades and at the back of my neck, brought on by tension.

Daisy Dayton was partially right. Tonight, at least, my nerves had taken a battering.

Nor was the situation likely to improve all weekend. Even if the dreaded motor-cycle invasion never came, I still felt threatened on a more personal level by the Starer.

Where had he come from? Where had he gone? Would he come back?

Probably he was nothing more than some dull little clerk in some grey anonymous firm, who would be horrified—and perhaps a bit flattered—to think that he could appear sinister at all.

The twinges between my shoulder-blades began to subside and I yawned as I neared the top of the stairs. Any danger was over, for the time being. I was back in my own digs, safely locked in for the night, surrounded by friendly people. I could relax.

CHAPTER 3

As usual, the floorboard creaked on the first-floor landing. I never seemed able to avoid it and it always startled me more than anyone else. Norma Handel would be sunk in slumber at this hour—at practically any hour—in the large front bedsitting-room overlooking the street. The other large room on this floor, occupied by Henry Parsons, the Punch-and-Judy man, was also dark and silent. He was another who had to pander to the caprices of a juvenile audience: perhaps that was what made him so aloof and morose when he was out of his sheltering booth.

The door at the far end of the hallway opened. I had a glimpse of a pale secretive face and a baleful eye, then a small hand shot out to close around a long handle attached to a flat disc and pull the whole thing into the safety of his room. Little Johnny was taking no chances that anyone might run off with his newest toy, a metal detector. But why had he left it out in the hallway in the first place if he was so concerned about it?

Shrugging, I climbed the final flight of stairs to the top floor, where I had the back room. The front room was

occupied by Kate Carter from the Mad Manic Music Hall.
Daisy Dayton did not entirely approve of Johnny's having
a whole room, even a small one, all to himself. However, I
quite saw Norma Handel's point. I wouldn't care to share
a room with Johnny myself. It was also kinder to the
child, since Norma only wanted to spend her time
sleeping, to let him have a place where he could watch
television, play records and entertain his friends—if he
had any. Although I doubted that Norma had been
worrying about Johnny's comfort.

'Oh, it's a sad thing, dear, very sad,' Daisy had confided to
me, soon after introducing Norma Handel and her young
son. 'She isn't one of us, of course, but I'm not prejudiced. I
don't insist on theatricals, although I'd rather have them.
Well, you know where you stand with your own, don't
you, dear? But I had to take them in, it's so sad. Besides,
she's a long-term boarder. That's not to be sneezed at,
these days. And she's warm, dear, very warm.'

I must have looked puzzled, for Daisy elucidated.

'Money, that is, dear, bags of it. Although not hers, not
yet. That's why she's got to toe the line—her mother-in-
law's line. She can't help it. The old lady has the money.
Norma's husband is *up there*, you see—'

My face must have shown that I didn't see. I glanced
heavenwards involuntarily, but Daisy Dayton hadn't been
referring to anything that high.

'In the Nursing Home—although I don't reckon *he's* con-
valescing. He's there for the rest of his days, if you ask me.
Just sitting in a chair staring into space, they say. Doesn't
recognize her or the boy when they visit him. Doesn't talk,
doesn't move. Oh, it's terrible, dear, terrible. And she's
still a young woman, she should be out enjoying herself.
But she never will—that mother-in-law of hers will see to
that. She's got to behave like a proper wife, even though
the man she married doesn't exist any more. But she's got
to live near by and go up and visit him twice a week, taking

the boy with her. It's not good for either of them, dear, not good. The only one it can't harm is the husband himself because he's beyond it all. But if Norma doesn't behave the way her mother-in-law thinks she ought to, she'll never get any of the money. No, nor Little Johnny, either. Oh, it's wicked, dear, wicked.'

I was inclined to agree. But I didn't feel that Norma Handel's attitude was helping. This was obviously the biggest crisis she had ever faced in her life—and she was coping with it by trying to sleep her way through it. At the cost of ignoring her son. It did not appear to have occurred to her that she might be laying the groundwork for another serious crisis in the future . . .

As I entered, my room was lit briefly by the sweeping beam from the lighthouse at the end of the marina. I didn't bother to put the overhead light on, but crossed to the desk at the window looking out over the back garden and the town. I stretched out my hand to switch on the desk lamp and hesitated, caught by the feeling that something was vaguely wrong and trying to identify what.

The bulb was still warm. The lamp had been switched off only recently. Someone had been in my room. *Perhaps he still was.*

I snapped on the light quickly and whirled around. The room was, of course, empty. If I hadn't been overwrought already, I would have known who the intruder had been. Realization came to me as I turned back to my desk and saw the untidy pile of unopened letters beneath the desk lamp.

Dear Little Johnny had been on the prowl again.

I crossed the room and opened my closet door. Sure enough, my suitcases were no longer quite as I had left them. Doubtless Johnny had moved them, the better to run his metal detector over them in search of hidden treasure. Why go to the effort of combing the beach when he might find something exciting closer to hand?

I slammed the closet door shut, certain that Johnny would be listening and get the message. If the noise disturbed anyone else, it was just too bad. It was high time something disturbed Norma and brought her back to reality; trying to join her husband in his catatonic state wasn't doing anyone any good.

I went back to my desk and took up my letters. There was a scorch mark on the back of one envelope where Johnny had pressed it against the light bulb too closely and too long as he tried to read its contents. I opened it and was pleased to see that it was a lined envelope—no wonder Johnny had been trying so hard to read through it. He must have thought it was something particularly juicy. In fact, it was a rather boring missive from my mother relating the uninteresting adventures of distant relatives I could barely remember.

The rest of my afternoon post consisted of letters from friends, a small cheque from a recording company for the one and only record I had ever cut, and an assortment of junk mail my mother had inexplicably forwarded, each enclosed in a fresh envelope, by air mail.

I set aside the only letter I felt like answering, took my keys out of my handbag and went back to the closet with the other letters. I used my empty suitcases as repositories for items I didn't care to leave lying about the room. Which meant practically everything—especially personal mail. I had learned about Little Johnny fairly early on in my residence here.

Daisy Dayton was aware of the problem and usually very good about locking up behind her when she had finished cleaning the rooms and making the beds. Unfortunately, she was easily distracted and an unexpected telephone call could bring her flying down from another floor; a prolonged conversation could disrupt her schedule so that she tended to rush on to the next task, neglecting to go back and clear up any unfinished items—like locking doors.

I opened the nearest suitcase and threw in the opened letters with unnecessary force. There was nothing in them that anyone could not have seen. They would have been a bitter disappointment to Johnny had he been able to read them. No secrets, no scandals, not even anything of any particular interest. All he could have learned about me—already visible from the address on the envelope—was that my real name was Gertrude Candowski. I had shortened it to Trudi Kane for professional purposes—a common practice. Nothing I could possibly be black-mailed over.

I wasn't sure where that thought had come from, or when that suspicion had begun to grow. Perhaps it was those sly watching eyes; perhaps it was the fact that Johnny always seemed to have so much money to play with. More than even the most doting mother might think fit to lavish on him. Not that I was certain that Norma had that much money to throw around. The general impression was that her mother-in-law, who *did* control the family money supply, kept her on a pretty short leash.

I relocked the suitcase and placed it in the far corner of the closet. I'd have another word with Daisy about keeping my door locked. My life might be an open book, but I reserved the right to be choosy about who turned the pages.

I went back to the desk and sat down to read the letter from Marge, who had taken over on the piano bar for the summer at Sandy Acres Bay. It was full of local gossip, bringing back familiar scenes. For a moment, I was looking out on the wide sweep of sea and sand dunes, seeing the familiar faces gathered around my piano. The 'summer people', who came back year after year; the wives and children moving into rented beach houses for the summer while their husbands sweltered in the steaming cities, working during the week and getting away at weekends to join them by the sea. They had been doing it for years, would continue to do it until the children were old enough to disappear into worlds of their own, leaving their parents free to make that trip to Europe—or get a divorce.

It was a way of life, if only for the time being. And I had watched them sitting around the bar in the evenings, the women in whatever was fashionable that particular summer, the men in their standard seaside uniforms, either jeans and T-shirts or Bermuda shorts and Bleeding Madras jackets, staring into their drinks and wondering where all the bright promise had gone. Where had Camelot disappeared to? How had the Sweetheart of Sigma Chi evolved into the Battleaxe of the Leavittown Estate? Would a new job, a new house, a new wife, bring back the magic?

I'd been on the gin-mill circuit for five years and there were times when I felt the general disillusionment was beginning to get to me, too.

Then, right at the end of the summer season, Ted had come along. His arm still in a plaster cast from the August raid, he had come to the States for a short holiday while his pub was being rebuilt. He'd wandered into the cocktail-bar where I was appearing one night and we'd started talking.

On the whole, I had no regrets. I was seeing a bit of the world; I got up to London about once a week and took in a matinee; I had even made a few day trips to France, although I had not got as far as Paris yet.

For the rest of it, I was an entertainer and a job was a job. I might just as well be playing the eighteenth chorus of '*Maybe it's Because I'm a Londoner*' of an evening as the eighteenth chorus of '*The Whiffenpoof Song*'. On the whole, the English were a more cheerful audience, less introspective and more genuinely out to have a good time. Cheerfulness breeds cheerfulness and I was finding renewed enjoyment in my chosen profession.

Also, I was a novelty here and that helped. If there

were any piano bars in England, they were few and far between. Ted had immediately recognized that I could be the starring attraction The Phoenix needed to become the most popular Lounge Bar on the Coast. He had arranged a Work Permit for me and imported me, piano bar and all. He was right.

At first, the customers had found it strange, and perhaps a little alarming, to be so close to an entertainer. The curved padded counter built around the piano had been deserted more nights than not while the customers had huddled at tables at a respectful distance. But gradually they had grown accustomed to it and begun to sidle into seats at the far end of the keyboard, until finally every seat was filled — even the ones right beside me.

After that, I found I could chart the progress of their holiday. The newcomers sat timidly at the rear tables watching the drill. As the incumbents around the piano rounded off their holiday and disappeared, I noticed that the others crept forward; from the rear tables to the front, from the front tables to the seats round the piano bar — giving every indication of enjoying themselves hugely at their own daring.

Apart from this principle, which I had learned was called 'Buggins's Turn', they behaved generally much as an American audience. They sent over drinks for the pianist and I always had a row of glasses ranged above the keyboard. Luckily, I also had the usual arrangement with Ted so that, despite the appearance, few of the drinks were actually alcoholic.

They also learned the method for requesting special numbers and I was soon swamped with the customary snow-drift of cocktail napkins and beer mats, sent up from the floor, with favourite song titles scrawled on them in ball-point, Pentel and even lipstick.

It began to seem almost like home, except for the vari-ation in titles and the fact that a few of the cast of characters were missing. I still got the amateur vocalists — some of them very good — who joined me at the microphone to sing their theme songs, but the amateur musicians were missing. Perhaps they were all working in groups over here, or perhaps rock backgrounds had left them un-equipped to cope with arrangements that depended on melody. At home, there was always a drummer. Some managements even kept a set of drums behind me so that punters who fancied themselves as Gene Krupa or Ringo Starr could have a go. Sometimes they showed up with their own drums. I didn't mind. They were usually content to thrum out the beat quietly in the background and it takes a lot to put me off. It hadn't happened here yet.

Anyway, Ted was pleased and talked of extending my engagement through the winter. Even better, interested parties from London had been down and were making discreet noises about London appearances in the Lounge Bars of exclusive hotels. It was too early to tell whether that would come to anything, but I smiled, nodded and trilled out with the fancy bits whenever I suspected some-one had slipped in to look me over.

So far, nothing had happened, but it was early days yet. A lot of the relevant people were still on vacation, flinging themselves as far afield as Inland Revenue were likely to countenance, heedless of talent right under their noses, if not exactly local.

Meanwhile, *The Stage* had mentioned me approvingly and the *Variety* correspondent had been close to lyrical. My future prospects were looking a lot brighter than the view had been from Sandy Acres Bay. Whatever else dis-turbed me about this engagement, I must remember that and hang on until something solid actually materialized.

I made a mental note to have another chat with Daisy Dayton about keeping my door locked at all times. I would stress again the undesirability of leaving anything unguarded with Little Johnny in the house. Daisy already knew this, but had an ostrich-like ability to hide herself from unpleasant facts. I suspected that Norma was paying rather over the odds for her accommodation — and for the illusion that her son was being safely looked after while she slept her life away. She was old enough to know that nothing was as easy as that and money couldn't buy quite everything. But that was Norma's problem, not mine.

I unlocked a desk drawer which bore telltale scratches around the lock and dipped into my stock of incredible seaside postcards which I had bought in an unbelieving daze when I first arrived. There was no need to keep them under lock and key, of course; similar examples were displayed in every shop along the front, but I still had the double-standard feeling that an innocent child should not be exposed to them. Of course, an innocent child shouldn't be rummaging through my room, either.

I chose one of the boldest and addressed it to Marge at Sandy Acres Bay, scrawling an indecipherable signature on it. If the US Postal Authorities let it through, she would know the source. If they didn't, they could never prove it was me sending such material through the US mails. Nations had double standards, too.

Just before I turned in, I drew the curtains, although the beam from the lighthouse was already blurred by the encroaching mist. The foghorn had started up, as well. A lot of people would be sleeping easier tonight when they heard it. It portended just the sort of weekend they had been hoping for: wet, murky and very discouraging to trippers.

I found that I, too, was feeling more relaxed as I drifted off to sleep with the foghorn still hooting direfully in the distance.

CHAPTER 4

Traitorously, Saturday morning dawned bright and beautiful. I was awake early and the first one down to breakfast—apart from Little Johnny, who had already eaten and gone out. I silently thanked heaven for that. Little Johnny Handel was not a person I wished to see across the breakfast table first thing in the morning. In fact, I could face it with equanimity if I never saw him again in my entire life.

At least he was out of the way this morning. For such small mercies, I was duly grateful.

'You're down early, dear.' Daisy Dayton hurried in with a pot of coffee and a guilty look, although it was I who should feel guilty for disturbing her early-morning session with the radio and the morning newspaper. 'I've just put your egg on to boil.'

'That's fine, thank you,' I said resignedly. I had long since given up trying to peruade her that I didn't really want an egg, only coffee and toast. I was paying for full board and full board I would have—if it killed me. We had compromised on a boiled egg and extra toast for breakfast, although Daisy still seemed to feel that she was cheating me because the others had what she called 'a proper fry-up', which consisted of various combinations of bacon, eggs, tomato, mushrooms, sausages and fried bread. To placate her, I managed the full breakfast on Sundays but, during the week, even one boiled egg was more than I felt like eating. Fortunately the cats were friendly and obliging; they didn't even fight over who was going to get the egg, but queued up to take a spoonful of egg in turn.

But we were all foiled this morning. Daisy brought in a

cup of coffee for herself, along with my breakfast, and sat down opposite me. Perhaps it was just as well. It would give me the chance to discuss our joint problem—even at the price of eating my own egg.

'Daisy—' I said, giving the importunate Formby a surreptitious push under the table with my foot; Robey and Fields had got the message when Daisy sat down and had retreated across the room to gaze benignly at the table with apparent unconcern— 'Daisy, I'm afraid you're going to have to do something about Johnny Handel. He's been in my room again.'

'Oh no,' Daisy sighed. 'No.' She seemed to be denying the need to take action more than the news that the brat had been on the prowl again. 'I'm so sorry, dear. He didn't take anything, did he?'

'Not so far as I can tell,' I admitted. 'I don't seem to have anything he likes. Fortunately.'

'He's never taken anything yet.' Daisy was more prepared than I to look on the bright side. 'It isn't as though he's a sneak thief—'

'Just a sneak.' I was not going to let her off the hook. 'He's been through my things. I don't happen to have anything worth stealing. But someday—'

'I know, dear, I know.' Daisy shook her head. 'That boy will come to no good end!'

'And the sooner, the better,' I said grimly. 'I won't have it, Daisy. You've got to keep my door locked—'

'It was!' she wailed. 'I've kept *all* the doors locked all summer—even on the hot days when I'd ordinarily leave them open to air the rooms properly. But it's no good. He's got hold of some sort of master key somewhere—and I can't be in the house every minute. I have to go out and do the shopping.' She seemed on the verge of tears.

'I just don't know what to do, dear. Honestly, I don't. There's no use changing the locks. It would cost a fortune and I couldn't afford it. And it wouldn't do any good as long as he's got that master key . . .'

'And it's no good talking to Norma, I suppose. Even if you could shake her out of that stupor.'

'She doesn't want to know, dear. She never did. And I hate to worry her, she's having a hard enough time.' Daisy looked at me fearfully, as though I might issue an ultimatum she didn't want to hear.

'I don't usually take non-pros, dear, you know, but this was different. They came personally recommended — just the way you did. Of course, you're a pro. But you know what I mean, I can't turn them out. It wouldn't be wise to upset Councillor Tiverton. He isn't a nice man when he's crossed, not nice at all.'

I could well believe it. He wasn't a particularly nice man even when he was trying his best to be charming. If crossed . . .

'Yes,' I said. 'I see what you mean.'

I wondered if I saw more than that. Councillor Albert Tiverton had never struck me as the type to take a disinterested attitude to damsels in distress. If he was prepared to do anything to alleviate their present distress, it was a pretty safe bet that they could look forward to a more personal distress in the future, when he presented his bill. If there wasn't anything in it for Our Albert, he wasn't going to play. The fact that Norma was able to lose herself in the sleep of the just for at least eighteen out of the twenty-four hours merely indicated that Albert Tiverton had not yet put in for payment.

'He's an old friend of the family, dear,' Daisy said defensively. 'Well, through his wife, that is. I've known Milly and Ted for more years than I like to recall. Naturally, I wanted to do them a favour when I could.'

'Naturally,' I agreed, giving Formby another push.

'Poor Milly,' she sighed. I thought for a moment she had homed in on my suspicions about the Councillor, but she was off on a tangent of her own. 'She thought she was doing so well, marrying a politician, but it just goes to show, doesn't it, dear?'

'That's right,' I agreed absently, lost again. I usually got lost at some point in any conversation with Daisy. Eventually, I either caught up with her or she moved to another subject; either way, it could be a merry chase. But I was still too annoyed this morning to play that little game.

'But the problem under discussion—' I called her back to order sharply— 'is Johnny Handel. Little Johnny Handel,' I added, just in case she might think I had someone else in mind.

Formby gave a sharp, despairing howl of frustration as he watched me swallow the last morsel of boiled egg. Daisy looked as though he had expressed her sentiments exactly.

'Oh yes, dear,' she said unconvincingly. 'Yes, of course. I'll do something about it, dear. I'll speak to him, I'll speak to him severely.'

That and ten pence would get her a ride on any bus in town.

'You do that,' I said uncompromisingly. 'I don't want him in my room again. There's no reason why he should even be on the same floor as my room. If I ever again find that he has been—'

'I'll take care of it, dear. I'll see to it.' She cut off my abortive threat hastily, which was just as well. I'd had no idea how I was going to end up. It was one of those sentences which, once launched upon, seems to carry its own momentum until, suddenly, you realize there's nowhere for it to go.

'See that you do,' I said darkly and stood up before I could get further embroiled. 'I'm going out now—'

'Going anywhere nice, dear?'

It was the sort of inane inquiry that always made me want to reply, 'No, I'm going somewhere nasty.' Where did they expect I'd be going?

'Shopping,' I said weakly, and fled the room with her words of encouragement winging after me.

'That's right, dear. You want to get to the shops before the trippers get there and pick everything over . . .'

Actually, I was only heading for Marks and Spencer's to pick up an attractive lambswool cardigan I had mentally earmarked for myself a couple of weeks ago when the new line had gone on sale. Daisy's warning was timely; I had already noticed how quickly popular lines sold out. There was something about the seaside air which caused the visitors to snap up items they could equally well find in their chain stores at home.

My stroll down to the shopping centre of the town was slowed by the constant flow of traffic which meant that I had to go out of my way to a corner where there were traffic lights before I could safely cross. I had never seen such a snarl of bumper-to-bumper traffic. And it was still quite early—not ten o'clock yet. By mid-day, the flood would have assumed terrifying proportions.

This was the last big weekend of the year. August Bank Holiday. The end of the summer school holiday for the kids, which is the reason the seaside is always so crowded for the month of August when parents take their holidays to fit into the school holiday. This weekend was the end of holiday for them and, for the trippers, a long weekend and the last chance for a whoop-up and knees-up between here and Christmas. They were all determined to make the most of it.

Inevitably, there were motor-cyclists among the crowd, but they seemed to be arriving singly or in pairs. Unless they were going to link up to form that terrorizing gang later. Townspeople on the pavement watched them suspiciously, which was hardly surprising. Their very uniform, especially the ominous hooded crash helmets, dehumanized them, turning them into robotlike creatures from whom anything might be expected.

I was nearly at the intermediate level containing the shops now. As I waited to cross the last street, the coaches began rolling past, placards in their windows identifying them so that their parties could recognize them easily in the coach park.

With eyes as mistrustful as any of the townspeople, I watched them roll past, mentally assessing their potentiality for carrying trouble. Three had parties of children who looked inadequately supervised. That meant the possibility of shoplifting and hooliganism. The more exclusive shops had already posted notices reading: 'Children not admitted unless accompanied by an adult'; but the shopkeepers along the promenade, specializing in sweets, ices and small portable novelties, were just going to have to take their chances with sticky little fingers.

Another coachload proclaimed itself The Darby and Joan Club, while another was a Senior Citizens' Outing. They seemed unlikely to get into any punch-ups although, these days, one could never be sure.

The traffic lights changed to red and the traffic growled to a reluctant standstill. The little green man flashed on and I started to cross the street. I was only half way across when he began to flicker warningly. I increased my pace and just made it to the kerb as the front line of cars leaped forward with an impatient roar. I hoped the older day trippers were pretty nippy on their feet, or there would be carnage of a different sort than expected this holiday weekend.

The shops were full of familiar faces as the townspeople did their shopping early to get in supplies, for the next two days when food stores and chain stores would be closed. I saw Milly Tiverton pushing a wheeled basket full of vegetables and salad greens. Ted walked beside her, carrying his own shopping which seemed to have pretty much duplicated hers. Although the deep-freeze for The Phoenix kitchen was always well-stocked, I knew that he considered it an admission of failure to have to dip into it for his own personal supplies. He had been a widower long enough to insist on demonstrating his ability to survive and live well without a woman in the house. I suspect that it was partly reaction against his sister's matchmaking attempts, which had never produced a female he considered satisfactory.

('Lame ducks, every one of them,' he had confided to me once. 'Speaks well for Milly's tender heart—she'd like to see the poor things with a happy ending. But she never seems to think what it would be like for me. I'm the one she bloody expects to live with them, as well as support them! Maybe she thinks it doesn't matter to me. Maybe she thinks I'm past it. Ah, well,' he had sighed deeply. 'Never mind. Let it be . . .')

It had crossed my mind even then that the reason all of Milly's friends were lame ducks might be because they were the only ones it was safe to have around with a husband like Albert Tiverton, but Ted had obviously never thought about that. If he had, he had ignored the thought. Perhaps he thought Milly was 'past it'. Siblings were never very good judges of each other's attractiveness or emotions.

Fortunately, they were on the other side of the street, so conversation wasn't required. I waved cheerfully and dodged into Woolworth's. I could use some toothpaste and soap.

What I couldn't use was a meeting with Little Johnny Handel. We realized simultaneously and with apparently equal horror that we were on a collision course in the toiletries aisle.

We both swerved abruptly, avoiding each other's eyes, and continued on our separate ways. He was heading for the door and I stopped in front of the toothpaste display to browse and try to decide whether I wanted to stick with an American brand I knew or try one of the unknown English quantities. It was the sort of decision I could normally spend a happy quarter-hour over, but now I could not settle to enjoying it. I had the uneasy feeling that Little Johnny might double back on his track and re-appear at my elbow momentarily.

I glanced over my shoulder and saw him, just as he was glancing back over *his* shoulder. He hesitated in the door-way, his expression both furtive and triumphant, then his eyes met mine and his face went blank. He turned and rushed out of the store, leaving me oddly disturbed.

Of course, Little Johnny always looked furtive. Usually with good reason, I suspected. Especially this morning— and not just because I had so nearly caught him going through my room last night.

I realized suddenly that, as he had come down the aisle towards me, I had received the distinct impression that he was stuffing a small unwrapped object into his pocket.

Perhaps I was wronging him and he had actually paid for it. But I didn't think so. This store usually put every item—no matter how small—into a paper bag. That, with a sales slip, was the customer's proof of purchase. I doubted that Johnny could produce a sales slip for what-ever he had put into his pocket.

There was nothing I could do about it. He was already out of the store and probably half way across town by now. Even if I reported my suspicion—and it *was* only a suspicion—he could have disposed of the evidence before anyone caught up with him. I also had the suspicion that he had had plenty of practice.

Nor was there any point in trying to talk to Norma about the problem. Even if she believed me, she wouldn't thank me for that sort of information. It wasn't what she wanted to hear. More probably, she wouldn't hear it at all. She would listen sleepily, not really assimilating any-thing that had been said to her, then yawn and go back to her room and her bed. To sleep some more, to while away the hours, days, weeks of waiting. Waiting for what?

Sleeping Beauty was traditionally awakened by a kiss from Prince Charming, but Norma had already found her Prince Charming, married him, and lost him to a deep trance of his own in one of the nursing homes on the top of the hill. Did she think that another one might come along if she retreated into the classic role? She forgot that fairy tales strictly rationed Prince Charmings: one per Enchanted Princess, till death do them part.

But Life was real, Life was earnest—and Norma was due for a rude awakening some day. Perhaps some day very soon. Police in the parlour . . . Little Johnny, tearful and protesting improbable innocence . . . Norma, blinking and yawning and wondering what had gone wrong with the script . . . none of the bit players knew their proper roles—and Prince Charming was nowhere in sight.

I hoped I wouldn't be there to see it, but I was dreadfully afraid that I would be. Life was surging on much too swiftly, as it always did. Only Norma seemed to have the gift of sleeping it away.

But the Summer Season was ending; the Pantomime bad spirits were gathering, snarling and snickering in the wings, ready to snatch away the gifts bestowed at the christening by the good spirits. If Norma didn't wake up soon, it would be too late.

Perhaps it was too late already.

CHAPTER 5

It hadn't been much of a day to begin with, and now it was well-nigh ruined. Before noon, even. Perhaps Norma had the right idea: it didn't pay to get up at all.

Thoroughly dispirited, I made my purchases at Woolworth's and plodded along towards Marks and Spencer's. It simply confirmed my gloomy loss of confidence in the entire day that the next person I ran into was Kate Carter from the Mad Manic Music Hall playing at the Grand Theatre at the end of the Pier.

Don't get me wrong. Kate is a darling, really. It's just that one gets the feeling she's typecast in her show— 'manic' is the word for it. After a while, one begins to hope for the depressive phase to set in, but it never does. There are a lot of them in show business and sometimes they make it big—very big, indeed. But, after the first half-hour, they can be very exhausting company.

'Trudi!' She hailed me from a drugstore, waving wildly— not so much to attract my attention as to dry the nail polish, a different colour on each nail of her left hand. 'Come and tell me what colour suits me best. I can't decide!'

'They all look marvellous.' I wasn't going to be drawn into that one again. I'd fallen for it before. Under the guise of soliciting advice, Kate managed to give herself a free coating of nail polish from the tester bottles—right under the eyes of the sales staff—in different stores about once a week. 'Why don't you buy the lot?'

'I might, at that,' she said, then hesitated. 'But which one should I *wear* tonight?' Abstractedly, she started on the nails of her right hand.

'Wear them all,' I advised recklessly. She usually wound up with a few mismatched nails, anyway. It wasn't easy to keep dipping into the same bottle with a salesgirl watching. 'Who's going to notice? You're up on stage. Your audience is far enough away for anything subtle to be lost beyond the first few rows.'

'Yes, you're right.' She sighed heavily. 'Oh, Trudi, you don't know how lucky you are, not having to work matinees.'

'I've got a pretty good idea,' I said. Since I didn't go on

duty at the piano bar until six—half an hour after opening time, in order to give a bit of an audience time to assemble—I had dropped in and sampled some of the matinee performances of the Summer Shows on offer. I'd found them pretty incredible.

A lifetime of summers heretofore exposed to the Straw Hat Circuit had left me totally unprepared for what the British considered suitable summer entertainment. Whereas America was dotted with Summer Theatres who vied with each other from June to September to bring the best available theatre to summer residents, the British seemed to consider that none of their audiences had an attention span beyond the traditional twenty minutes allotted to primary school children. American offerings varied from the tried-and-true old standards to pre-Broadway tryouts of new shows. The British Summer Shows were mostly revues, largely consisting of the kind of acts that killed vaudeville.

After viewing a couple of them, I began to long for the sophistication of *Springtime for Henry*. Not to mention the weary expertise of whatever superannuated actress was currently touring in *The Glass Menagerie*. I even longed for the gaucheries of the no-hoper tryouts allegedly bound for Broadway, even though everyone knew they'd never get any farther in that direction than the Manomet Playhouse. At least, these all presumed an audience willing to engage themselves for the evening through two acts and an interval. Another plus was that you seldom saw children at these performances. An American summer audience wanted to escape from its brats for an evening, not drag them along with them.

'*And* your audience is over eighteen!' Losing interest in nail polish, Kate replaced the last bottle in the rack. She now had a complete manicure, albeit a somewhat eccentric one. It went with her image, though, and she seemed quite happy about it. 'You don't know what an advantage it is not to have to pitch your act towards the dear little kiddies, as well as their Mums and Dads.'

'I've got a pretty good idea,' I said again. Most of the acts I had seen flop did so in the no-man's-land between the generations. Some 'artistes' just about ruptured themselves trying to get the jokes blue enough to make an X-rating, in the hope that the adults would laugh, while the reason for the laughter went over the heads of the little darlings in the audience. Few succeeded. Most limped offstage to reluctant applause, leaving behind a strained atmosphere as parents hoped the kiddiewinks would forget to demand an explanation of the jokes later.

'Not while you're protected by the Licensing Laws, you haven't,' she said bitterly. 'You'll never know what it's like until you get Our Own, Our Very Own, Little Johnny Handel in the audience heckling you. He'll probably be there this afternoon. God! Someday I'm going to murder that little bastard!' She flexed her multi-hued talons wistfully. 'I'd be a public benefactor. They'd give me a medal.'

'Every performer in town would contribute to it,' I assured her. I had heard Little Johnny's lovable habit discussed at length over the supper table. The Great Dandini dreamed of getting him onstage to help with the Sawing-the-Lady-in-Half routine and bundling him into the box instead of the lady, and then forgetting the part of the routine essential to the safety of the body in the box. The Punch-and-Judy man favoured the simple blunt instrument technique and swore he kept an iron bar in reserve inside his booth, ready to use it at the first opportunity and lay the blame on Punch. But Little Johnny was too clever for any of them and remained out of range, yodelling catcalls and bright remarks from the back of the audience.

'Never mind.' She was still gloomily contemplating the prospect of this afternoon's matinee and I tried to cheer her. 'The Season is coming to an end. This is the last big weekend of the year. He may get bored with that amusement when the audiences aren't so big.'

'It's not so good for us, either, when the audiences shrink.' Kate helped herself to a generous dollop of hand lotion from another tester. 'It means they may not bother to keep us going until the end of September if the returns aren't worth it.'

'Surely they wouldn't close it down. Anyway, you've got a contract—'

'Run of the Season,' she said gloomily, massaging the lotion into her skin, giving the impression of wringing her hands. 'I didn't like that wording to begin with. It doesn't define the length of the Season. If the Corporation decides the Season's over, there we are. They'll close the show on the grounds of saving the ratepayers' money and we won't have much comeback. Oh, we'd get Equity to fight it out with them, but it would probably end in a compromise. Meanwhile, we'd be out of work. And it's a long time until the Christmas Pantomimes go into rehearsal."

'It may not happen.' We left the counter and moved out into the street. I headed towards Marks and Spencer and she came with me, obviously having attached herself to me for the rest of the morning.

'On the other hand, it may be on the cards now.' She was determined not to be cheered. 'Councillor Tiverton has dropped a few hints, you know.'

'I'll bet that's not all he hinted.'

'You're right.' She grinned suddenly. 'Isn't it too bad he isn't as important as he thinks he is? I don't want to be caught within ten miles of him when his balloon bursts.'

'What do you mean?' This was the second time this morning I'd heard strange intimations about Councillor Tiverton. I couldn't decide whether it was a matter of general knowledge I'd missed out on because I hadn't been in town all that long, or whether it was something peculiarly English, the nuances of which would for ever escape an American.

'Oh, nothing.' She shrugged restlessly. 'He's not worth worrying about. To hell with it! To hell with everything!' She straightened her shoulders, her chin shot up defiantly. 'I've come to a decision. Do you know what I'm going to do? I'm going to put the Massage Parlour Skit into the show this weekend!'

'You can't!' I gasped. She had performed it for us on Sunday evenings at the digs. It was killingly funny, but awfully close to the knuckle. And, for a seaside audience, with children included . . . 'You'll never get away with it. They'll ring down the curtain.'

'I'd be well into it before anyone realizes—and then they won't dare.' She laughed aloud. 'Just watch me! I mean it, Trudi. Come along to the matinee and witness the Great British Premiere.'

'I'll do that,' I said. It would be interesting and instructive to see how the sketch played before a mass audience. And she might just get away with it. After all, the show was called the Mad Manic Music Hall—and I'd never seen anything as mad and manic as that skit. Also, Kate was shrewd enough to temper her material to the mood of her audience. She had never played the skit in exactly the same way twice, even for us; it was bound to change and improve if she could work in front of a live and critical commercial audience.

Kate had several sketches she had devised and written herself. They were sharp and funny—perhaps too sharp; they seemed to stir the audience to uneasiness as much as to laughter half the time. She had begun by using 'Air Hostess' in the Music Hall ('I'm sorry, the wing seems to have fallen off. But don't worry . . .') It brought instant identification with everyone who'd ever been on a package tour. When she had realized this, she had immediately begun work on 'Tour Leader' and introduced it.

('Your husband went off to find the Black Market to change some money and hasn't come back yet, Mrs Badger? Three days ago? . . . Of course we'll look into it. Meanwhile, let me introduce you to Mr Henley. His wife went round to the kitchen last week to complain to the chef about the food. He hates being on his own . . .')

Her other sketches were too sophisticated for her present audiences. She'd do well in cabaret or supper clubs, perhaps even better in a one-woman show. The problem, as with all of us, was making the breakthrough.

'Be careful!' In her abstraction, Kate had nearly stepped out into the stream of moving traffic. I pulled her back. 'Watch where you're going!'

'Sorry,' Kate said. 'I was lost in thought,' she added, unnecessarily.

'This is no place and no time to think,' I scolded. 'You'd better stay on your toes this weekend. The town is full of strangers who don't know where they're going but don't want to waste any time getting there. It's dangerous.'

'I know.' She shuddered and looked around, taking in the hordes of holidaymakers crowding the street, their voices raucous and complaining, already looking for places to eat. 'I hate it when the town is like this. Too full, too crowded with people just down for a day or the weekend. I suppose it's good for business, but I still hate it.'

'So do I,' I agreed. There was something unnerving about so many people milling about without any purpose except the vague amorphous one of having a good time. It gave a curiously rootless feeling to the whole town: all these people, surging through, determined to enjoy themselves, as though they were making a smash-and-grab raid on happiness.

And sometimes it was other people who got smashed.

DID YOU SEE THIS GIRL? The police poster shrieked from shop windows, from the Tourist Attractions Bulletin

Board, from lamp-posts and hoardings. The face of the dead girl stared out with blank sightless eyes betraying the fact that it was a death photograph. Perhaps somewhere she had featured on holiday snapshots, live and laughing.

But not here. Here, she had been the 'August Nude', the body on the beach after the August Holiday tide had receded. She was 'This Girl', still unidentified after all these months. The police had obviously rushed through this batch of new posters in the hope that someone who had been here last August Bank Holiday might be paying a return visit. Probably their hopes didn't extend to the murderer's returning to the scene of the crime; they would be satisfied with any fragments of information which might help them to construct a picture of her last day on earth. Someone who had glimpsed her on the promenade, or buying something in one of the shops, or perhaps exchanged a few words with her and had noticed whether or not she had an accent, either foreign or regional. Perhaps, if they were very lucky, a witness who had seen her with someone else and could describe that companion. The odds were astronomical, but the chance had to be taken. Meanwhile, the blank eyes stared out at the passing throngs, most of whom just glanced at the poster and glanced away again. It was nothing to do with them.

'Ugh!' Kate followed the direction of my gaze and saw the police poster. 'That was a nasty do. Why do they have to drag it up all over again? And on a Bank Holiday weekend, too!'

'Because it's still unsolved, I suppose. They think someone might remember something. Another Bank Holiday weekend—it's a psychological time to joggle memories. You were here then, weren't you?'

'Yes.' She gave a sharp, almost hostile look, obviously reading more into my innocent question than I had intended. 'But all I know about it is what I read in the

48

papers. We were breaking in a new act in the Mad Manic Music Hall that weekend, so we had enough troubles of our own. Then, when the motor-cycle gang arrived—' She broke off and shuddered. 'I don't *want* to remember that weekend. No one does. Why can't they let it be?'

I had already answered that question. I remained silent.

'We were *all* here then,' she said defensively. 'All except *you*.' She made it sound like an accusation. Tit-for-tat, I suppose. She seemed to think that I had been blaming her in some way. 'It was the last big holiday weekend of the Season. That's why the town drew so many visitors.'

Two motor-cycles roared past us, snorting defiance at the world. Kate flinched visibly.

'Sorry,' she apologized, 'but I hate those things. I wish they'd never been invented.'

'That's hardly surprising. Most of the town feels that way. And yet, it's only a minority who misuse them. Most of the cyclists are decent, law-abiding people who can't afford to run motor-cars.'

'Then let them stay home!' Kate spoke savagely. 'Or at least use public transport.' She shuddered again. 'I'm sorry, Trudi. But you don't know what it was like that night.'

'I've heard quite a lot,' I said, and I had. From Ted, nursing both his broken arm and his drink as he sat beside me at the piano bar, telling me of the horror, but trying to persuade me that it was unlikely to happen again and I ought to come and spend a season working at his new pub.

From Daisy, who had sat in her own living-room watching with incredulity as the television set relayed the incredible scenes of vandalism and devastation from the sea front just a few hundred yards below. ('I didn't let the cats out for a week after that, dear.')

From the townspeople and shop owners, who had made Ted's new pub their gathering-place in a gesture of solidarity with the local resident who had suffered most during the invasion. Also, of course, The Phoenix was the newest, brightest and best pub along the promenade. They seemed to like my act, too.

From the other performers, who had been caught in the midst of the violence and looting as they tried to make their way back to their digs after their shows had ended. I knew for a fact that several of the more high-strung had already provided themselves with tranquillizers in dread anticipation of this weekend.

Like the survivors of earthquake, blizzard or other natural catastrophe, everyone had their own story of that weekend. Where they were, and what they were doing when the motor-cycle mob struck; the narrow escapes, the bruises, the insults, the terror. One and all dreaded a return engagement.

'We were lucky,' Kate said. 'Dandini and I were still in the theatre at the end of the pier. We just stayed there all night — the whole cast. When the first motor-cycles began to race each other along the pier, the manager pulled up the drawbridge. They didn't expect that — most of them didn't know it existed. A couple of them shot right off into the water — *that* cooled them off. And ruined their machines, too, I sincerely hope!'

'Served them right,' I applauded. 'Too bad the shop-keepers along the promenade weren't so well fixed.'

'We stood at the end of the pier and watched the fires they set. It was unbelievable, like something out of a night-mare.' Kate was shivering, despite the heat of the sun. 'They were savages — from another world, another time. You could *feel* the hatred. Especially after they lost those four machines. They splashed around in the water, cursing us. And you should have seen the faces on the others as they climbed down the pilings to help them salvage the machines.' She gave another deep shudder.

'That's why I'm afraid they'll be back. They want revenge.'

CHAPTER 6

It had developed into one of those rare days when an English theatre could have done with air-conditioning. Such days are few and far between — and so are English theatres equipped with air-conditioning, although the heating systems are usually adequate. They need to be.

In the afternoon heat, the audience had been uncomfortable and restless, myself included. Released now from the matinee performance, I breathed the cool salty air gratefully. The length of the pier stretched out before me, leading back to the promenade and I decided to let the crowd go ahead of me. I sat on one of the free benches (there was a charge for using the deck chairs) and relaxed.

The crowd headed for shore as eagerly as their Victorian counterparts must have done. The difference was that they had approached this end of the pier from the shore, whereas the Victorians had arrived by pleasure steamers from the great smoky cities, disembarking with gratitude at the end of the pier. With gratitude, because the steamers were unable to sail in close to shore and, prior to the building of the long proud piers the length and breadth of the English shoreline, disembarkation at the seaside resort of their choice had meant that they had to climb down into smaller boats that would take them in closer to the shore; the final stage of their landing being accomplished piggyback astride porters who carried them on to the beach safely and reasonably dry. Small wonder that vaporous ladies and their stiff-necked escorts soon opted for those resorts which built landing piers jutting out into the water to meet the steamers half way. Before long, every seaside town had boasted its own pier and the great Victorian exodus to the seaside had begun.

It continued to this day, but now by dry land all the way. From my vantage point, I could usually see the day-return coaches discharging their passengers at the bus stop just beyond the pier. It was too late in the day for that now, of course, it was nearly time for the coaches to begin picking them up for the return journey home.

Those around me were already demolishing the last of their picnic lunches. Along this end of the pier and at the back of the theatre, fishermen hopefully dangled their rented lines in the deep water, waiting, with a patience that bordered on coma, for a bite. Seagulls wheeled above, ready to swoop on any crust that might be thrown away.

The tide was going out and the foreshore seemed to lengthen every time I looked at it. Some people were still swimming, but more were paddling, trouser-ends rolled up, splashing in the shallows. Children were still building sand castles or playing with frisbees; most of them. I spotted one who was intent on more serious things.

Little Johnny Handel was sweeping the shore with his metal detector. That child had a one-track mind—and profit was the track. Yet, according to Daisy, there was no lack of money in that family. Obviously, he felt that enough of it wasn't filtering through to him.

I was too far away to hear the buzzer go off, but I saw him halt abruptly, then slowly and meticulously swing the metal detector around in a long arc. Several of the other children abandoned their games and sidled closer to him, watching intently.

Johnny raised his head to glare at them and they fell back. Not far enough. He waited, pulling the metal detector close and clutching it to him. His lips moved. Whatever he said could not have been pleasant. The children moved farther back.

Still not far enough. Johnny remained motionless, glaring. They all held the tableau for another minute, then, suddenly, the children broke and scattered, fleeing back to the safety of sand castles and frisbees.

Johnny watched them go, waiting until they had resumed their games. When they were all occupied, not even glancing in his direction any more, he began to move slowly. In his own way, he was as patient as the fishermen along the pier. But there was something unnatural about such patience in a boy of thirteen.

Almost surreptitiously, he began swinging the metal detector in that slow arc again, in ever-decreasing circles until he seemed to find what he was looking for, almost at his feet. He sidestepped, stooped, and began burrowing in the sand.

When he stood again, brushing sand from some small object, satisfaction was radiating from him. He stuffed the object into his pocket and went to work with the metal detector again, quartering the relevant area as professionally as a search-party. Clearly, he felt that there was more to find.

From this distance, I could not see what he had uncovered. I could tell, however, that he was very pleased with himself, so it must have been something of value. Intrigued, I watched as his search progressed.

'Oh, Trudi—' I jumped as the unexpected voice spoke at my elbow. 'I'm so glad you waited for me.' Kate was looking down at me eagerly. 'What did you think of the sketch?'

'Umm . . .' I tried to look as though I were considering my answer. Actually, I hadn't given it a thought, but I could hardly admit that. Nor did I feel I could go into the 'Darling, you were marvellous' routine which keeps most performers happy. Kate was a cut above that. True, she wouldn't spit in my eye if I did say it, but she would be hoping for an honest answer. Not quite so honest as the truth, though. Besides, I had been thinking about the act— while it was going on.

'You changed it a bit,' I said slowly. 'Watered it down . . .'

'With that audience, what else could I do?' She heaved an exaggerated sigh. 'I knew they weren't dead—I could hear them breathing. And rattling sweet wrappers. And passing the time of day with each other. I don't know why they bother to pay the admission charge if they're going to ignore the show. It isn't as though it was raining today.'

'They *were* awful.' I was able to agree unreservedly. 'It was the heat, I think. They aren't used to it.'

'It will be better tonight.' She cheered up. 'Cooler. And not so many kids in the audience. I'll let rip then. Too bad you won't be able to see it.'

'Never mind.' I stood and we began strolling back along the pier. 'I'll catch another matinee—after you've broken it in a bit. Then you'll have a better idea of how it's going. By the end of the Season—'

'*If* the Season lasts another month, the way it's supposed to,' she interrupted. '*If* the yobbos don't come back this weekend and burn down the rest of the town.'

Automatically, our eyes turned to the sea front. It looked much the same as usual, except that the crowds were thicker and livelier. It was, of course, impossible to tell whether there was latent hostility and incipient rioting lurking behind the animation. By the time we knew that, it would be too late.

We had nearly reached the promenade when I became aware of that familiar prickling sensation at the back of my neck again.

Someone was staring. At me.

I halted abruptly and Kate stopped, too, puzzled. 'What's the matter?' she asked. 'You've gone quite pale. Aren't you feeling well?'

'No,' I said shortly. Trying not to be too obvious about it, I began scanning the pier, turning slowly. No one in the immediate vicinity appeared to have any interest in me. Very well. I widened the area of my scan.

'Do you want to sit down? I could go over to the café and get you a cup of tea. You're not going to faint, are you?'

'No.' There was no one behind me on the pier, no one ahead on the sea front, who was paying any attention to me at all. Of course, there might be someone watching from behind the curtains at one of the upstairs windows in the self-catering holiday apartments over the shops along the front.

'Well, you're looking a little better now,' Kate conceded. 'You're sure you don't want to sit down and rest for a minute?'

'No. Thank you. I'm sorry, Kate, I just—'

And then I saw him. Standing below on the beach, glaring up at me. Relief flooded me.

It was only Little Johnny Handel. A second later, I wondered why I felt such relief. If it had been an adult staring at me with the same implacable hostility, I would have been frightened.

'That brat again!' Kate followed the direction of my gaze and made a face. 'At least he wasn't at the matinee today. I suppose I should be grateful for small mercies.'

'No,' I said. 'He's been playing on the sands with his new toy, that metal detector.'

'Norma spoils him. Those things are expensive. And he'll only get bored with it before long. It will be tossed aside, just like all his other expensive toys.'

'He seems interested enough in it at the moment,' I said, which was not strictly true. He seemed far more interested in me—but not in any pleasant way.'

'He's glaring at you.' Even Kate had noticed it. 'He seems in an absolute fury. What on earth have you done to him?'

Caught him shoplifting this morning. Or *almost* caught him.

But I could not say that. I had no proof. Only an instinctive certainty which would never stand up in a court of law. Kate would believe me without proof, of course. But she would also talk about it. That way lay trouble—plenty of trouble. Even the dormant Norma could be roused like a tigress to defend her cub against an accusation like that.

'I don't know,' I said feebly. 'He just seems to have a grudge against the whole human race. I suppose you can't blame him too much. Even though Norma seems to buy him everything he wants, he's still getting a pretty rough deal from life.'

'I blame him,' Kate said firmly. 'I'd blame him for anything. After all, plenty of other kids have had a rough deal in life but they don't go around acting the way he does.'

'Some of them act worse,' I defended, although I hadn't really much interest in playing devil's advocate for Johnny Handel. 'Look at the ones who leap on to motor-cycles and ride out and beat up towns.'

'Give him time,' Kate said. 'That will probably be Johnny's next step. I'd say he's well on the way to it now. As soon as Norma is fool enough to let him have a motor-cycle, he'll be hell-bent for leather with the rest of them.'

It was only too probable. Only his age and the laws of the land kept him from it now. As soon as he was old enough, there'd be no stopping him. Where once rebel children dreamed of running away and joining a circus or the gipsies, Johnny Handel would dream of joining Hell's Angels—and he was a prime candidate.

'Come on.' Kate pulled at my arm. 'We can't stand here and hold a staring match with him. Besides, you'd never win, you know.'

'I know.' Johnny could outstare the Sphinx. As I turned away, he moved at last. He lifted his arm, doubled his fist and shook it at my back, not aware that I had caught the gesture from the corner of my eye. It was a pretty international gesture.

Well, okay. What did I care for his opinion of me? He wasn't my favourite person, either.

The quickest way off the pier led through the amusement arcade. It was possible to get on or off the pier without passing through, but it wasn't easy. The alternative route was a long curving detour skirting the featureless outside of the arcade building. No doubt it had been carefully arranged this way, since the City Council had had a great deal to do with the building and siting of the arcade. They weren't ones to let the punters have a chance to keep any change in their pockets.

We strolled through the dark aisles assaulted on all sides by whooping electronic noises. Microchip-powered Space Invaders warred with traditional rifle-shooting booths where the targets were untraditional three-dimensional laser beam projections. All the wonders of modern day science harnessed to a coin pay slot to pull in the suckers' loose cash.

There were also the perennial old favourites, the fruit machines, incorporating the fairly recent innovation of the Nudger button, to give the punters the spurious illusion that skill might have something to do with their chances of winning. If they could just learn to Nudge at the right moment.

A particularly English favourite was the Penny Falls, although few of them could be worked for a penny any more. Two pence was the going sum, with five-pence and ten-pence machines creeping up. It was new to me. The money rolled down a chute to land on a level constantly brushed by an upright partition moving back and forth. If the coin fell in the right position, it was then pushed against the mound of other coins already on the shelf, dislodging some of them to drop down to the next level, where the process was repeated. If the player was lucky, a few coins—or an occasional landslide of coins—fell into the payoff cups at the bottom of the machine.

There seemed to be a constant queue of children at most of the machines, and quite a few adults, too. There was no minimum age limit for players. If a kid was big enough to shovel money into the coin slot at the top—even if it had to stand on its toes to do so—it was old enough to play the machine.

The English were infected with gambling fever at an early age. No wonder there were betting shops on every city street corner.

'Whew!' We emerged into the sunlight, blinking and trying to shake off the semi-hypnotic state induced by the darkened arcade, the weird sounds, the gambling fever all around us. 'There's something frightening about those places.' Thank heaven for daylight again.

'Oh, this one's all right,' Kate said. 'Unlike some I could mention—' She broke off abruptly, as though discretion had suddenly set in.

I decided to let it pass. I was vaguely aware of sinister rumours about a couple of shadier amusement arcades down at the seedier end of the town, but this was not the moment to pursue the matter. So far as I knew, there had never been any open scandal and the march of progress would inevitably take care of such places. When the Marina was completely finished, that sort of sleazy rundown property would be in too valuable a position to be allowed to remain. Some enterprising merchant would take it over, tart it up, and run a reputable line of merchandise from it.

The problem would solve itself, given time. Whereas, other problems . . .

Involuntarily, I glanced over my shoulder. Johnny Handel was following the tide line as the tide went out. He had moved in closer to the metal struts supporting the pier, despite the fact that they seemed to be driving his metal detector haywire. But he appeared to be able to

58

sort out the different messages.

As I watched, he stooped and began digging in the wet sand.

'Come on,' Kate said. 'You want your tea before you go to work, don't you?' She glanced at me anxiously. 'You're sure you're well enough to work tonight?'

'Yes,' I said. 'I'm fine.'

CHAPTER 7

The Phoenix was crowded and noisy. I had been practically standing on the loud pedal for the past half-hour in order to make myself heard over the hubbub. On the off-chance that there might be a few customers who were actually interested in the music. It didn't seem particularly likely tonight.

As usual, the more uninhibited of the clientele were clustered around the piano bar, but even they seemed more interested in each other than in the entertainment. It was Saturday night with a vengeance.

At least, the Saturday-night Starer wasn't here. Not yet. Maybe he wouldn't show up at all. Maybe he'd got his fill of whatever strange kicks turned him on last night. Maybe.

Ted had stationed himself near the door and was inconspicuously vetting the customers as they arrived. He'd refuse admittance to any undesirables—if he could spot them in time. Sometimes they started out all right but underwent a personality change after a few drinks. You couldn't always tell. Most of them just got rowdy, or perhaps extra affectionate, but a few, a very few, turned really nasty.

For the moment, everything was fine. My audience, although not particularly attentive, was appreciative, as the row of glasses ranged above the music rack testified.

Had they really contained Gimlets, I'd have long since been under the piano. But Ted and I had the usual arrangement and no one on the floor could tell that they were only lime juice; what Ted charged for them was his business. It was all part of keeping the customers happy—and some of them watched closely to make sure I actually drank the drink they'd sent up to me.

On the shelf beside the music rack, the pile of paper cocktail mats and napkins was growing. Each had a request for a special number scrawled on it, some written out neatly in ink, complete with 'please' and 'thank you'. Others were written in blunt pencil, the paper caught and torn as someone bore down heavily to make the writing dark enough to be read. A few were from couples who obviously never felt it necessary to carry writing instruments around with them and were scrawled out in eyebrow pencil or lipstick.

I usually managed to play most of the requests during the course of an evening, interspersing them with my regular numbers. This, too, was part of keeping the customers happy.

I picked up the top napkin: some nostalgic customer wanted to hear 'Some of These Days'. That was easy enough. What threw me were the requests for songs from English homegrown musicals which had never reached Broadway or received any American attention at all. Deservedly, I had realized when the local amateur theatrical society had performed a couple of them earlier in the season. Although the lyrics were occasionally sophisticated enough in a would-be Cole Porter manner, the tunes were usually tinkling, simplistic—and unfortunately reminiscent (just this side of plagiarism) of too many American hits of that era. Many of them were also pitched far too high, written for the sort of soprano voice that has disappeared from the modern musical stage.

Of the plots, the less said the better. They all seemed to

be laid in mythical kingdoms so that the principals could strut around in crowns and jewels, the men in gaudy uniforms, the women in glittering tiaras and dresses with long trains, with a large cast of jolly adoring peasants dancing around. Perfect for amateur musical societies, but no wonder they'd never been seen in the States. American producers might occasionally be stupid or have lapses into bad judgement, but they weren't totally suicidal.

Nevertheless, I had begun haunting music shops, book stores and antique/junk shops looking for old scores and sheet music to repair the deficiency in my repertoire. It had become a hobby and I was amassing quite a collection. The old musicals might be inept, but there was the occasional good song, and a lot of the old Music Hall songs were quaint enough or funny enough to be good material for American supper clubs today. The suspicion was growing at the back of my mind that I was on to something here.

Automatically, I had been rippling from one number to another, sometimes singing, sometimes just playing the melody. It was an easy audience tonight, prepared to treat me as musical wallpaper. Sometimes they were as fractious and demanding as children wanting Mummy's attention. Even those sitting up at the piano were absorbed in each other rather than in me. Almost unconsciously, as I went through my routine, I had been watching Ted.

Now I saw him twitch uneasily and frown. He was still watching the doorway and I followed his gaze. The reason for his unhappiness was quickly apparent.

Councillor Tiverton swept through the doorway as though he were about to address a political rally. Arm-in-unwilling-arm with him, pinioned close to his side, was Norma Handel. For once, she looked almost awake . . . and frightened.

Lips tightening, Ted moved forward to meet them. His

brother-in-law shook Ted's hand as heartily as though he were a constituent who could throw a few thousand votes in his direction. Ted looked grimmer than ever.

Smiling blandly, Councillor Tiverton started for one of the tables for two in a dark corner of the room. Ted and Norma acted in concert. Ted blocked his path, Norma tugged him in the other direction—towards me.

Giving in with fairly good grace, Councillor Tiverton turned and bore down on the piano bar, tossing me an electioneering smile as he looked for a couple of empty seats.

That was all I needed tonight: the end of a perfect day.

' 'Ere—watch it!' The little blonde Cockney sparrow on the stool nearest the keyboard did not take kindly to having the Councillor's ample stomach rammed into the small of her back. Who could blame her?

'Is 'e givin' you trouble?' Her escort rose and, I was happy to see, towered over Albert Tiverton. He looked as though he might be something in the heftier end of the building trade. 'Just you watch it, mate!'

'Sorry—' Councillor Tiverton turned his vote-catching beam on the man. 'I thought you were just leaving.'

'Well, we're not!' He continued to hover truculently over the Councillor. 'So, suppose you just 'op it!'

I noticed that Ted had turned away and was rather ostentatiously taking no notice of the scene. I got the impression that anyone who wanted to thump his brother-in-law would be able to get in quite a few good punches before Ted was moved to intervene.

'Sorry. No offence.' It wasn't going to happen this time. Councillor Tiverton gave the man a placatory smile and moved back.

Norma sent me a wan smile.

'Good evening, Trudi.' He turned his attention to me.

I nodded and gave a frosty smile. I wasn't going to vote for him, either. One night when the bar was crowded he had tried to come round the barrier and sit beside me on the piano bench. We weren't going to have a repeat of that performance.

'You're in fine voice this evening.' He continued to press, implying an intimacy which didn't exist. 'Just what the doctor ordered. That's why I brought this poor young lady along—' From the pained expression on Norma's face, he had squeezed her arm with more strength than was necessary.

'Can't have her sitting at home brooding on a Saturday night when everyone's out enjoying themselves, can we? Not when she's got such an unpleasant duty ahead of her tomorrow—' He lowered his voice so that the announcement only reached those around the piano bar and at the immediate tables.

'It's the day she goes to see her husband. In one of those places at the top of the hill. Nothing to look forward to, poor child. Ah, it's tragic . . .'

A couple of sentimental idiots got up from the piano bar and gave him their seats. I could have killed them.

'Thank you. That's very kind of you. Have one on me—' He signalled to Ted, who was alert again now that the danger had passed and was keeping a disapproving eye on him.

Trying to ignore all the byplay and give the impression of being deeply absorbed in my work, I picked up the next cocktail napkin, and frowned, trying to decipher it. English handwriting is in a class by itself—several thousand classes, in fact. Americans are taught their nice uniform Palmer Method and have no idea how grateful they should be for it. Over here, every child is left to go its own way and the resultant chaos is somehow considered properly individualistic—even though it might be unreadable. The writing surface of a paper napkin didn't improve matters.

At last the hieroglyphics shifted and formed themselves

into some semblance of order as I blinked at them desperately: '*The Eton Boating Song*'. Good. That was one of the new numbers I had learned since coming to this country. I even liked it.

As the melody rippled from my fingertips, I was prepared to bet that, for every battle won on the playing fields of Eton, several more battles had been lost because no one had been able to interpret the handwritten battle orders correctly.

'Here! What do you want to go playing that rubbish for?' Now that he had his ringside seat, Councillor Tiverton was prepared to take over as Master of Ceremonies. His sort was another occupational hazard. 'Give us something lively, so we can have a sing-song. That's what we want on a night like this, eh? Get the party going!'

He could go at any time and I wouldn't mind in the least. I wouldn't even mind if he took Norma with him. She looked ready to fall asleep sitting upright. Unfortunately, such a means of escape wasn't open to the rest of us.

'Come along now—' Councillor Tiverton raised his voice to rabble-rousing pitch, obviously under the mistaken impression that he was being the life and soul of the party. 'Something bright and jolly everyone can enjoy. Something for all these lovely people who've come to our happy town to have a good time—and the best place in the Kingdom to come!' He raised his voice still higher and broke into song, drowning out the piano completely.

'Oh, I *do* like to *be* beside the seaside . . .'

The Cockney couple closest to me decided to let bygones be bygones and joined in.

'Oh, I *do* like to be beside the sea . . .' Other voices took up the refrain.

If you can't beat them, join them. I fumbled for the right key, then decided it didn't make any difference, everyone was singing in a different key anyway. Loudness was all that was required.

I gave up and tried to throw myself into the spirit of the song although, strictly speaking, I was not beside the seaside: I had my back to it. The piano was placed so that the customers would have the view. Everyone could look out over the promenade, the sea and the lighted pier except me. I could have been in any bar from here to Hackensack. Only the accents were different, and I was noticing those less and less as time went on.

The song came to a rowdy ragged end and there was an outburst of applause. Well, if that was what the customers wanted, I'd give them one for the home team. I swung into:

> *By the sea, by the sea,*
> *By the beautiful sea . . .*

They took it up enthusiastically. Looking more amiable, Ted brought over the drinks for his brother-in-law and Norma and then took orders for refills from most of those around the piano. He nodded approvingly at me and crossed round behind me to stare down at the promenade through the large plate-glass window for a moment before returning to the bar.

It was time for my break, so I flipped on the tape in the cassette beside me on the piano bench before I got up and paused at the window to speak to him before disappearing into the staff room.

'Seems to be going well,' I said.

'Aye.' He nodded, still searching the promenade for signs of impending disturbance. 'Could be worse. Still plenty of time for trouble to break out, though. I'll be glad when this season's over. One way and another, it's been a bad year.'

There was no answer to that. From what I had heard, he was right. In any case, I had no previous English criteria by which to judge it.

I nodded sympathetic agreement and was about to move away when I saw him suddenly stiffen and freeze. At the same moment, the skin between my shoulder-blades began to creep and shrivel. I followed the direction of his gaze and saw that he was staring down at a small slight figure silhouetted against the blaze of lights outside the amusement arcade where the pier joined the promenade.

Not the Starer, though. This figure was female. Blonde. Lost-looking. She might have been a ghost—or a revenant. The victim, returning to the scene of the crime. I knew that thought must, inevitably, be in Ted's mind.

'Perhaps the police are doing a reconstruction,' I said quickly. 'She may be a policewoman they've sent out to try to jog people's memories. In case someone who was here last August—'

'Not bloody likely, darling!' An over-familiar hand descended on my shoulder and began insinuating itself down towards forbidden territory. My flesh crept in earnest now. I moved away abruptly.

'Couldn't possibly do a reconstruction. They don't know what the girl was wearing when she was alive.' Councillor Tiverton seemed to be addressing only his brother-in-law, ignoring me. 'She was starkers when she was found. Only way any of them had ever seen her. Couldn't send a little policewoman out like that, could they? The Chief Constable wouldn't like it. No Lady Godiva monkeyshines here. This is a respectable town. Or was.'

For the first time it occurred to me that no town with him in it could be completely respectable. Especially not one which had voted him on to the City Council.

'No. Only one person could ever say what she was wearing—' Councillor Tiverton shot a sly glance at Ted. 'Her killer. Dirty bugger stripped the clothes off the poor lass and took them away with him. Who knows what he did with them? Maybe he burned them in the furnace—the weather was still cold enough that week for all the fires to be lit. Or maybe he's kept them as a sort of souvenir, to take them out and look at them, maybe stroke them and—'

Ted swung away from the window, hands twitching as though they would like to reach out and close around his brother-in-law's throat. I wondered suddenly what he had done with his late wife's wardrobe.

'Ted!' I spoke quickly, without thinking, but it checked him.

'Yes. All right.' He did not seem to be speaking to me. He let his hands drop, but still faced his brother-in-law with hostility. 'Where's Milly?' he asked.

'At home.' Councillor Tiverton appeared slightly less at ease. 'You know how she is. Wanted to do some cooking, holiday weekend and all.'

'I know how she is.' Ted's voice was heavy with meaning. 'I know how you are, too. Why don't you cut along home to her?'

'Here now, is that any way to talk? When I've dropped in to add to your takings? And brought along a poor creature who needs cheering up?' Councillor Tiverton glanced over his shoulder, then did a double-take.

Norma was gone.

'She's got more sense than you have,' Ted said. He looked down at the promenade, but there was no sign of Norma. The girl who had been standing in the pool of light gave a brief upward glance, as though aware that she was under unwelcome observation and melted away into the shadows.

I caught my breath. For an instant, there had been something devastatingly familiar about her. Not the face—that had been just an indistinct blur as she turned it upwards—but . . . The identification eluded me. She was not anyone I had ever met. Had I seen her picture somewhere? . . . On a police poster?

I gave myself a mental shake. More probably, she was someone who had been into The Phoenix and sat round the piano one evening. That might account for the almost-recognition. How many people had crowded round the piano during the three months I had been appearing at The Phoenix? After a while, they all seemed to dissolve into the same face. Few of them were as memorable as they thought they were.

In fact, their clothes were more recognizable than their faces. Thanks to the multiplicity of chain stores, all carrying the same lines, in every corner of the country, women's wardrobes tended to be nearly identical when there was an especially popular line. Unlike the States, where different stores and designers at least tried to ring a few changes when a fad for a certain garment swept the country.

I realized abruptly that that was why the girl had looked so familiar. It was not her, it was the flowered blouse she was wearing. I owned a blouse like that myself. It had been high style a couple of seasons ago, sweeping all before it, from Paris to Seventh Avenue. It had evidently been a success in this country, too. The best is always international — or almost always.

'Oh Christ!' Councillor Tiverton suddenly went rigid, staring over my shoulder at an apparition in the doorway. 'Christ!' he muttered again.

I turned, half-afraid of what I might see. But it was not the ghost-girl from the promenade standing in the doorway, nor even yet the Starer. The doorway was filled with the all-too-solid form of Milly Tiverton. She was carrying a large covered dish and she turned slowly, looking for someone.

Albert Tiverton cast a guilty, frantic glance towards the piano bar. Norma's seat was still vacant. True, a half-finished drink marked the place, but there was no possible way anyone could know whose drink it had been.

The Councillor relaxed visibly. A slow, sly smile slid across his face as he realized that, no matter what his intentions had been, he had actually been caught doing nothing more incriminating than having a quiet chat with his brother-in-law and the resident pianist.

'Over here, love!' he called out, suddenly brazenly cheerful. He waved extravagantly at his wife.

Milly's face cleared and she crossed the room to us. 'I won't stay, Ted,' she said. 'I know it's a busy night. But I thought I'd just bring these along for you. What with the long weekend, I was afraid you might be running low.' She tipped back the tea-towel to reveal three quiche dishes, set one on top of the other.

'I've done a smoked salmon flan,' she said. 'A spinach, and an egg-and-bacon. That ought to see you through. If you don't need them tonight, you can put them in the fridge for tomorrow.'

'That's lovely, Milly,' her brother said helplessly. The crowd had long since lost any interest in food and settled down to serious drinking, the evening was winding to its close. 'Just what I need.'

'That's what I thought.' His sister looked at the crowded room with satisfaction. 'If you need any more, just let me know.'

'That's right,' her husband said, a trace of rancour in his tone. 'She'll do anything you want. All you have to do is snap your fingers.' He snapped his own, in illustration, then looked over his shoulder nervously, as though he feared the gesture might summon Norma back to his side.

Behind him, the door to the Powder Room opened and a girl came out with a worried expression on her face. She paused and looked around the room, as though seeking help.

'Well, come on, love.' Albert Tiverton took Milly's arm. 'You've delivered the goods. Time we were getting on—' He began guiding her towards the exit.

'Oh, stop a bit,' Ted invited wickedly. 'Have another drink. There's no rush.'

From across the room, the girl's eyes found Ted and she began moving purposefully in our direction.

'No, no. If Milly wants a drink, we'll have one at our next port of call. Farther along the front. I want to check a few more places before closing time.' Albert was pushing Milly towards the door now. 'You're all right here, but there might be trouble elsewhere.'

There was trouble here, from the look of the girl who was almost upon us.

Fortunately, Milly hadn't noticed. She was too flattered and flustered by what appeared to be her husband's sudden desire for her company. 'Albert wants to go,' she informed us unnecessarily. 'Perhaps we can stop another time.'

'That's right,' Albert promised recklessly over his shoulder. 'We'll come by and have that drink and a proper visit tomorrow night.'

'You do that,' Ted said wryly. 'Both of you.' He watched them leave before turning to the girl, who had now reached his side and was silently pleading for his attention.

'Pardon me,' she said uneasily. 'But there's a woman in there—' she waved vaguely towards the Powder Room. 'She's slumped in a chair. She's—she's awfully quiet. I—I couldn't even tell if she was breathing. Perhaps you ought to call a doctor.'

CHAPTER 8

Ted sighed deeply. It was Saturday night and almost closing time. There was always something. We walked over to the door of the Powder Room and he hesitated outside.

'Have a look, would you, Trudi? See what's the problem. I can't go barging in there—' He looked over his shoulder. The girl had gone back to her seat, but was watching us. 'Unless I'm certain it's an emergency.'

'Well, okay,' I said reluctantly. I wasn't so keen to go barging in myself, but I could see his point. It was probably someone who had just passed out. A nuisance, but a familiar nuisance. I took a deep breath and pushed open the door.

It was Norma.

I might have known it. That woman could sleep on a bed of nails, let alone in a chintz-covered well-upholstered armchair. I looked down at her without favour.

'All right in there?' The door opened a crack. 'Nothing really wrong, is there?' Ted's voice was fearful. A death on the premises was the terror of anyone in the trade. It gave a place an uneasy aura, not to mention the difficulties of trying to smuggle out a body unnoticed. And, in a place like The Phoenix, which had already been ravaged once by violence, it could mean the beginning of a reputation as a bad luck place. Not the sort of place the punters would choose for a pleasant evening. No wonder Ted was worried.

'It's all right.' I crossed to the door to reassure him. 'It's only Norma. She's fallen asleep again. I don't know why she bothers to get out of bed at all!'

'Just sleeping?' His face lightened. He turned and gave a thumbs-up signal to the girl sitting at the table. 'That's all right. Leave her be, then. I'll tip her into the car when I take you home. No more trouble to ferry two than one. Cheer up, won't be long now.'

'No.' I glanced at my watch. I was due back at the piano for my final stint; my entire rest period had been wasted with this nonsense. For a moment, I debated covering Norma, then dismissed the idea. If she didn't care, why should I? She was so far out of it, she'd never know the difference, anyway.

Nevertheless, her deep motionless slumber might alarm other customers. It had already frightened the last one into reporting her condition. A covering over her would signal that the situation was known and, hopefully, under control.

I found a blanket in the cabinet concealed behind the ruffled curtain in the corner. It also contained an extensive first-aid box and a sewing kit, in case repairs of any kind were needed. The events of last August had bitten deep into Ted's consciousness.

I tossed the blanket over Norma. She stirred, moaned and frowned, as though resisting any attempt to call her back to wakefulness. Unseen, I frowned back at her, then went out and left her there.

Norma passed me in the hallway the next morning on her way back to her room from the bath. She gave me a vague smile and I wondered if she remembered anything at all about the events of last night. Probably not. Everything must seem to be part of some insubstantial dream to her. She had evinced no surprise—or even interest—when she awoke briefly as Ted carried her down the stairs at The Phoenix and into the car; she had made the later transfer from the car into our lodgings without seeming to attain more than semi-consciousness.

Ted had been quite worried as Daisy opened the door. 'You don't think we ought to call the doctor?' he suggested. 'She hasn't taken pills, or anything?'

'Pills could take *her*,' Daisy said, with rare bitterness. 'I've never seen anything like it. Some days she doesn't surface long enough to have more than a cup of tea. No wonder—' She broke off. 'Where *is* Little Johnny? I thought he must be with her, at this hour.'

'Is he out running wild again?' Ted spoke with heavy disapproval. 'No good will come of that lad. If she doesn't care for herself, she might spare a thought for him, once in a while.'

Upstairs, as though on cue, a door opened. Too much on cue? Sharp ears listening behind a slightly ajar door, spying on the others in the house?

'Is that my mother?' He appeared at the top of the stairs, deceptively innocent in his pyjamas.

'Now, when did he come in?' Daisy muttered under her breath. 'I never heard him.'

That signified nothing. No one heard Johnny unless he intended to be heard. I had learned that at a very early stage.

He had descended the stairs, the picture of filial devotion and taken my place at his mother's side. 'It's all right,' he said nobly. 'I can manage her.'

I'd just bet he could—in more ways than one.

Norma had smiled in reflex action at hearing her son's voice, but hadn't bothered to open her eyes. She had leaned against Ted heavily as he and Johnny guided her up the stairs and into her room.

We watched them from the foot of the stairs and Daisy turned to me, shaking her head. 'I don't know, dear,' she said. 'I just don't know . . .'

But now it was morning, a bright new day. The crack of dawn for Norma to be up and bathed. Eleven a.m. Of course, it was visiting day at the nursing home for her—and Little Johnny. She'd probably sleep for a week after that.

As I descended the stairs, Robey and Fields stalked out from the kitchen to check on me. If only they could talk, Daisy might know a lot more about what went on in her own house. They kept their eyes on everything and everyone: proper watch-cats. But watch was the operative word. They stayed silent and thought their own thoughts.

Right now, they thought I wasn't half so interesting as

what was going on in the kitchen. They were right. Having registered my presence, they turned and went back to the scene of more interesting activity. I followed them.

'Going out, dear?' Daisy greeted me absently, her real attention centred on the onions she was chopping at the kitchen table. 'Don't stay too long. Lunch at one today, remember.'

'I thought I'd go down to the beach,' I said. 'The weather is so beautiful, I might take a swim.'

'That's right, dear,' Daisy approved. 'It can't last much longer. Enjoy it while you can.'

Fields leaped up on the table to check on what she was doing but leaped down again hastily, nose twitching in indignation at the reek of onions. She sneezed, then leaped up on the draining-board to lap up a bit of water from the sink. It was a sight to chill the blood of anyone who was a purist about hygiene, but we had always had cats at home. I would sooner see Fields's nose poked into things than, say, Little Johnny's.

'I'll be back in time,' I said, starting for the door. 'There's not much else to do *but* swim on an English Sunday — even if it *is* Bank Holiday weekend.' All the tourist traps and catchpenny stalls along the front would be open, but they didn't tempt me; they were for the trippers.

The telephone in the hall rang abruptly. Daisy couldn't have been more upset if a bomb had gone off.

'Oh no!' Her knife went clatering to the floor. She looked at the clock in agitation. 'She's too early today. Norma hasn't left yet. I can't talk to her. I can't!' She sent me a pleading look.

'You take the call, dear. Tell her I'm not here. I've gone out and you don't know when I'll be back. Tell her—' she added, with an air of triumphant improvisation— 'tell her I've gone to church!'

The voice on the other end of the line was cold and remote, with a cut-glass accent. I could understand why Daisy would be reluctant to speak to her at the best of times. Without even knowing her, I took a perverse pleasure in frustrating her attempt to get through to Daisy. She informed me frostily that she'd ring again later.

'Now what was that all about?' I went back to the kitchen. 'Who was that awful woman? And what was all that about Norma?'

'She *is* awful, isn't she, dear?' Daisy brightened at having what was obviously her own opinion endorsed. 'Simply frightful. I feel so sorry for Norma. I'd protect her if I could, but I can't, dear. Really, I can't. That was her mother-in-law. She calls every visiting day to check up on Norma and make sure that she *has* gone to the nursing home with Little Johnny to visit her husband. If she catches her missing a visit, she cuts off her allowance for that week.'

'That's barbaric!' I was shocked. This was the first time I had heard anything about these wheels within wheels. 'Surely Norma is old enough to decide whether she wants to go or not. From what I've heard, it doesn't make any difference. He doesn't recognize them anyway.'

'True, dear.' Daisy sighed. 'And making her drag that poor boy along all the time, too. It's wicked, dear, wicked!'

'I don't see why Norma doesn't rebel,' I said. 'She doesn't have to put up with that sort of thing in this day and age.'

'I'm afraid she does, dear. Mrs Handel has all the money. It's not just the allowance—she'll disinherit Little Johnny if Norma doesn't do as she wants. It's the old, old story, dear. The one who pays the piper is the one who calls the tune.'

'Poor Norma.' I felt a new sympathy for her. She had more to contend with than I had imagined.

'We're all ever so sympathetic, dear, but there's

nothing we can do to help her. I'd lie for her, if I could, but it wouldn't work. Mrs Handel rings the Matron at the nursing home after she's talked to me and makes sure that Norma has arrived and is with her husband. It's a private nursing home and a permanent patient like that means a lot of steady income. Matron tells Mrs Handel everything. *She* wouldn't lie for Norma, so there's no use me trying — I'd be caught out.'

'That's monstrous!'

'Quite right, dear, I do agree. Monstrous. Of course, Mrs Handel *is* rather a monster. I met her when she came to inspect the rooms before Norma and Johnny moved in. She wanted to see what they were getting for her money. And she was the one who insisted that they be served their meals privately so that they wouldn't have to mix with the *artistes*. I was awfully glad to see the back of her. Poor Norma!' Daisy sighed again. 'The worst of it is, dear, sometimes I think Little Johnny takes after his grandmother!'

'Poor Norma.' I echoed her sigh. Poor, poor Norma, caught between two of them. No wonder she was spending most of her life in Morphean retreat. 'If only she weren't so passive. She's still a young woman. She could get out and find herself a job. There must be something she can do.'

'Oh yes, she used to be a secretary, but it's not that easy for her, dear. Her mother-in-law wouldn't approve of that, either. The Handels don't work for a living, not like the rest of us. Norma's got to be careful for Johnny's sake. There's big money at stake there, dear, really big money. More than anyone could afford to throw away for some whim of independence — not that Norma is the type, anyway. All she has to do is hang on — the old lady can't last for ever. Then she and Johnny will get the money. Well, Johnny will, anyway — and everything will be all right.'

Would it? Little Johnny did not strike me as someone who could be depended upon to be generous to an indigent mother. If he held the purse strings, Norma might find herself dancing to even more stringent tunes. *Takes after his grandmother*, indeed. No matter which way you looked at it, Norma was storing up big trouble for herself in the future.

'Perhaps,' I said.

'Oh, I know what you're thinking, dear.' Daisy shot me a shrewd look. 'I've thought it myself at times. But all we can do is hope for the best. After all, it's nothing to do with us, really, is it?'

'Just as well,' I said. There were going to be an awful lot of pieces for somebody to pick up some day. Meanwhile, I still wanted to get down to the beach this morning.

'I've got to get going—' I started for the door, but stumbled over one of the cats, who ran in front of me, obviously hoping to dart out of the door when I opened it. 'Ooops! Sorry, George—I mean Gracie.'

'Oh, she's a one!' Daisy leaped gratefully to change the subject. 'Deceptive right from the start, she was. We called her Sid, at first. For Sid Field. But then she went and had a kitten, so of course she had to be Gracie.'

'We called the kitten Tony Hancock,' Daisy continued, reminiscing. 'He was a sweet little thing and very funny. But he ran right in front of a car and got run over. Perhaps we should have given him a different name. Poor Hancock always was suicidal, dear.'

I closed the door behind me softly, cutting off Daisy's memories. I didn't know whether she meant the kitten or the comedian at the last, and perhaps she didn't, either. As a change of subject, it was only slightly less depressing than Norma and Little Johnny. I felt that another day had got off to a bad start.

CHAPTER 9

The bleak uneasy mood stayed with me all the way down the hill and along the front. The row of bathing-huts were on the far side of the Grand Pier and seemed to be another particularly English institution, probably first conceived with and intended to be used in conjunction with bathing-machines. Hence, a Victorian lady could walk through the town fully and respectably dressed, change in the privacy of the family bathing-hut and then be conveyed direct from the door to the water in a bathing-machine without her more immodest costume being revealed to any watching eyes.

These days they were fighting for the right to have topless beaches, even nude beaches. The bathing-machine had become a complete anachronism, but the huts still lingered on, too useful to be dispensed with. They were basically a tiny one-room shack, windowless, but with a wide barn-like door. Inside there was usually a small sink, a clothesline to hang wet bathing suits from, and an electric connection for a hot plate or electric kettle so that no one need ever miss their cup of tea. After that, the contents varied according to the requirements and whims of the hut's owner.

The huts huddled together in a long row with scarcely an inch between them on either side. Most were rented out for the season, but some of the townspeople retained their own for private use.

Ted owned one close to the pier and there were several communal keys so that the staff of The Phoenix could use it, if and when they felt so inclined. Usually, I was the only one to take advantage of the privilege.

The day was colder than it had looked, a brisk wind

blowing in from the sea. I nearly changed my mind, but sheer bravado carried me through. I could not go back to the house and admit that I had skipped my swim because of a bit of a breeze. Besides, there might not be many more opportunities this season.

I didn't linger in the water. However, I was reluctant to return to the house. I wanted to wait until Norma and Little Johnny were sure to have left.

I pulled out one of the deck chairs and set it up outside the doorway, but changed out of my wet bathing suit before settling down in it. Behind and above me, I could hear laughter and splashing from the boating pool on the other side of the road. The customers were beginning to arrive and pop their kiddies into the little boats to get them out of their hair for a few minutes. Although it was not as popular with the children as the amusement arcades, it was better value for their parents. At least, the kids couldn't be shovelling coins into a machine while they were healthfully occupied in the open air pedalling a boat around the shallow pool.

I let the tattered paperback fall from my hand and lay back, closing my eyes against the sun. Whenever the wind dropped momentarily, it was really quite pleasantly warm. I felt myself drifting off into a doze.

Suddenly the background sound floating through the air changed character. The shrieks of laughter were transformed into screams of fear. Sharp as an electric shock, the change of mood jolted through the atmosphere, charging it with terror and unhealthy excitement.

I struggled out of the deck chair and hurried across the road. I was not the only one. Already, crowds were gathering at the perimeter of the pool, casual strollers rushing forward to view the sensation promised by the screams and cries.

I shouldered my way through to the railings where distracted parents were vainly shouting instructions to offspring in the boats now bumping together in the centre of the pool where the action was taking place. One and all, the children were ignoring the cries of distress and command. Only the pool staff could force the young mariners back to shore—and they were otherwise engaged, watched by a rapt and breathless audience. Even the frantic parental cries were stilled as the drama progressed.

Two attendants had climbed into the shoulder-high rubber waders they usually wore to clean the pool in the early hours of the morning. Grimly intent, they waded forward slowly towards the cluster of small boats. I noticed that, while the people on shore were looking out to the centre of the pool, the children were staring over the sides of their boats down into the water.

There appeared to be a bundle of rags bobbing up and down in the water. But no one would be so grimly intent upon retrieving a bundle of rags.

The ripples eddied out as the waders advanced, setting the body in motion almost as though it were trying to swim away from them. It bumped up against one of the boats and the children in that boat shrank back, nearly overtipping the craft by the swift movement of their recoil.

One of the men stretched out a hand and steadied the boat. The other caught hold of a handful of wet material and pulled the body towards him.

It rolled over lazily, wet blonde locks gleamed dully in the sunlight. The face was parboiled from overnight immersion in the water and had a pale blueish tinge.

Several of the children who had previously been silent in their boats screamed with terror and began sobbing. Suddenly it wasn't just an exciting adventure any more. Too much reality had crept in.

I felt rather that way myself. This was no unknown groupie left in the wake of a motor-cyclists' invasion. This had been a girl with a definite identity, a personality, a boy-friend who cared for her.

Although I could not put a name to her, I knew her face. It was the Cockney girl who had been sitting up at the piano bar last night.

I stared unbelievingly at the washed-out barely-recognizable face, paralyzed by the horror that seizes us all when we become aware that someone we have known — however peripherally — has been overtaken by a fate beyond our comprehension.

Only last night, she had been sitting at the piano bar, laughing with her boy-friend, annoying Councillor Tiverton, joining in the songs, lively, pretty, having a wonderful time. Today, she was nothing but a — a *thing* bobbing about on the surface of the boating pool while people recoiled from her in horror. Something to be pointed at, stared at —

People were even taking photographs. That was too much! What kind of people would want to capture this on film? And why? As the high point of their holiday snaps? 'And this is the actual discovery of the body. You remember that case — ?'

Why was I so sure it was murder? Because she hadn't seemed the sort to commit suicide? Because the boating pond was railed off from the general public and locked at night, which ruled out accident? Because the town had been tense and unhappy all weekend, waiting for something nasty to happen? There was very little that was nastier than murder. Had she been raped first?

I forced my eyes back to the body, but it was impossible, of course, to tell if her clothes had been disarranged. They were a wet sodden mass dragging down the body. Such questions would have to wait for an autopsy.

Suddenly I felt a cold prickle at the nape of my neck. I tried to turn as slowly and casually as possible, knowing what — who — I would find behind me.

It was the Starer. He stood on the fringe of the crowd, those avid staring eyes fixed on the body. He stared as though he were taking in nourishment through his eyes, while the men in the pool towed the body to shore by the boarding platform where a couple of uniformed policemen stood waiting. There was an obscure satisfaction deep in his eyes as they drank in the scene.

I shuddered. They always make me shudder.

What is it with these creeps? Once life was so simple. You became an entertainer because you wanted to make people happy. If you succeeded, Stage Door Johnnies waited for you with diamond bracelets wrapped around long-stemmed roses to whisk you off to champagne suppers at Romano's. If you really hit the top, students and admirers unbuckled the horses from your carriage and pulled it through the streets themselves. Those were the days!

These days they just want to kill you.

Perhaps the human race is evolving a deadly new mutant strain, the flesh-and-blood equivalent of the new technological advances in heat-seeking missiles, designed to home in on brightness and warmth — and destroy it.

I began edging my way out of the crowd, away from him. Performers have always had to cope with the side-effects of being in the spotlight. We've had to learn to deal gently with the problem portion of our audience: the misfits, the loners, the oddballs, the human strays who have somehow equated the spotlight with the party and imagine that, if they can just brush close enough to the lights and the laughter, it will somehow become their passport to everything they've missed in life so far. Some mysterious alchemy — like the Royal Touch which cured disease, or the Philosopher's Stone which transmuted base metal into gold — would inject itself into their bleak lives and transform them into sought-after members of the community. The Beautiful People, living on some unimaginable plateau of glory where the sun always shone, the champagne always flowed and the birds made music all the day.

They would feel short-changed and cheated if forced to realize that we also had headaches, got our feet wet in the rain, sometimes felt lost and lonely, frightened and inadequate ourselves. *If you prick us, do we not bleed?*

There was a splash and a shout from the pool behind me and I wished I hadn't had that last thought.

When I turned back, the Starer had disappeared. Had he stared his fill, or had he noticed my movement and feared I might be heading towards him? He needn't have worried. I was no more anxious to confront him than he was to come face to face with me. If we ever met, I wanted Ted between us, plus a couple of sturdy policemen.

Had the Starer been in The Phoenix last night? The new thought struck me sharply. I hadn't been aware of him, but he wasn't particularly memorable in his own persona. Probably, when he wasn't staring, he was as inconspicuous as ninety per cent of the audience. Would I have noticed him if he hadn't been staring?

Or if he hadn't been staring at *me*?

Had he, perhaps, been sitting at some point in the room from which his direct gaze would fall, not on me, but on the Cockney girl sitting close by me at the piano bar? Had she, by inadvertently intercepting his stare, somehow taken my place in his twisted mind?

Had she intercepted the fate intended for me?

CHAPTER 10

I was late back for lunch, after all, but Daisy forgave me in view of the eye-witness report I was able to give. This led to a lively mealtime debate over whether or not I ought to go to the police with the tiny fragment of information I possessed.

'I'd leave it be, dear, honestly I would,' Daisy advised. 'I mean, you don't even know the poor girl's name. You can't really be much help, can you? And as for reporting a man just because he's got funny eyes . . . Well, they might start looking at *you* pretty funny themselves. And you don't know *his* name, either, do you?'

'No,' I admitted. 'But the fact that the girl was in The Phoenix last night might provide a starting-point for the police enquiries—'

'And wouldn't Ted love that!' Daisy gave a mock shudder. 'They'd go and plaster one of their dirty great posters— HAVE YOU SEEN THIS GIRL?—right in front of The Phoenix. Put the customers off going in, that would. You couldn't blame them. It would be like walking into a place with a Plague Cross on the door. People want to have a good time, not be reminded of any awfulness around.'

'Daisy is right.' Henry Parsons speared another roast potato from the bowl in the centre of the table with the same motion with which Punch bludgeoned Judy into unconsciousness at the end of his show. Daisy automatically passed the gravy boat along to him. 'It can't do any good and it might do a great deal of harm. Keep out of it!'

'I don't know,' Kate said dubiously. 'You'd know him again if you saw him, wouldn't you? You might be an important witness.'

'Witness to what?' Dandini asked. 'Did she see the murder? Did she even see them together? All she saw was a man watching a scene dozens of other people were also watching. We'd be in a fine fix if the police could arrest a man for that. It's all anyone does in this town.'

'Our audience—' Kate lifted her glass in a toast. 'God . . . bless them!'

'Exactly, dear.' Daisy nodded sagely. 'It wouldn't do if it got around that you'd reported a member of your audience just because you didn't like the way he looked at you. Men can get awfully sensitive about things like that.'

'She's right,' Kate said. 'The punter probably thought he was giving you his best Robert Redford come-hither look. He'd be shattered if he knew the way you were taking it.'

I allowed myself to be persuaded. I didn't really want to go to the police with the nebulous fears and feeling I had about the situation. They'd laugh me out of the station.

Well, perhaps not exactly. This was England. They'd be excruciatingly polite to my face and laugh after I was safely out of earshot. The end result would be the same; they would not take my information seriously and, worse, I might become branded in their minds as some sort of eccentric or potential hysteric.

But I made a point of telling Ted about it before I started work that evening. I knew he'd take me seriously—and he did. He'd seen the Starer in action.

Not surprisingly, he agreed with the consensus of opinion. 'I've as much respect for the police as anyone,' he said, 'but it wouldn't be good for business to have them hanging around here. Start the customers worrying about breath tests—if nothing worse—and they'd cut down on their drinking. Then they'd start watching what they were saying and begin wondering if they'd have a better time in some other pub. No, it wouldn't do. The police have their work, we have ours. Let them get on with it and see how they go. You can always mention it later if they don't seem to be getting anywhere with their enquiries.'

'All right,' I agreed, sitting down at the piano and riffling off a preliminary introduction. 'Besides, the information probably isn't worth anything. She and her boy-friend might have been in and out of half the pubs along the front last night.'

Ted nodded, obviously not believing the rationalization any more than I did, but that would be our story in the face of any possible future criticism. Our eyes met in silent agreement and he moved away.

The Phoenix was beginning to fill up but no one had been bold enough to sit up at the piano bar yet. I was just as happy. It gave me a breathing space in which I needn't swap cheery comments or listen to snatches of other people's problems.

I gave the customers a long piano medley without vocal accompaniment and they seemed satisfied. More important, so did Ted. I could continue to save my voice for the moment, this was perfectly adequate music to drink by, soft and unobtrusive, familiar but not demanding, soothing as cool fingers stroking a fevered brow. The conversation level in the room was a hum of contentment. The customers were happy and enjoying themselves — which was just the way it should be.

I exchanged bright smiles with the first brave souls to seat themselves at the far end of the piano. I thought I had seen them here before, but could I be certain? Performers saw so many faces in audiences, along the sea front, in casual encounters with friends and acquaintances that, in time, everyone came to look vaguely familiar.

The ice being broken, other couples began to take seats around the piano. I kept a wary eye on them, wondering what I should do if the man who had been with the murdered girl last night showed up again tonight. Especially if he was with another girl. Should I report it to Ted? Would it be time to notify the police then? On the other hand, would I — could I — recognize him? Or had his face already blurred in my memory and mingled with so many others of the anonymous blurs that made up my audience? The girl had been the vivid member of that couple. Perhaps too much so for her own good.

I relaxed as the last seats were taken and it became apparent that I was not going to be faced with any such problem. There was a different problem, of course. It was one of those days.

The seats had been claimed by Councillor Tiverton—
who was escorting his own wife, for a change. Milly's
presence guaranteed that I would be spared the worst of
his leering attentions. He would be on his best behaviour
to make up for almost being caught out with Norma last
night.

'Now then, love.' The Councillor put an arm around
her with an air of demonstrating to all the other women in
the place just what they were missing. 'Choose your
drinks, choose your songs, anything you like. The night is
yours.'

I'll bet she hadn't heard that very often.

'Oh, Bertie!' She was delighted and dismayingly flattered
by it all. '*I* don't know.'

'Cocktails? Champagne? Brandy? Anything you like,'
he repeated expansively. 'And don't forget the music.
She'll—' he nodded his head dismissively at me— 'play
everything you want to hear.'

Actually I had a few other requests to fill first. The cocktail napkins bearing their scribbled requests were beginning to pile up beside the music rack. I couldn't devote
the whole evening to Milly Tiverton's choices.

Not that I needed to worry about it. Her mind had
obviously gone blank under the unaccustomed attention.
She would be hard put to remember her own name right
now, let alone any song titles.

I smiled at her encouragingly and continued with my
usual repertoire.

'Champagne cocktails!' Her husband impatiently decided for her. 'We'll all have one. The piano-player, too.'

Ted materialized behind them to take the order,
although a waitress was dealing with the other orders
around the piano. He returned to the bar to mix them
personally and then served them. I got the impression
that he wanted to keep a close eye on his brother-in-law.

Perhaps he mistrusted all the sudden solicitude for his sister.

I lifted the champagne cocktail—it was the genuine article—in salute and automatically segued into the 'Anniversary Waltz'. I had played this scene so often. Champagne cocktails equalled the 'Anniversary Waltz'; they were seldom ordered at any other time. It also explained why the Councillor was being so extraordinarily nice to his wife tonight.

It was a mistake. Tiverton's face darkened, even as Milly giggled. I saw Ted repressing a smile.

'No!' Tiverton scowled at me. 'It's not an anniversary. And it's not a birthday, either. Can't a man and his lawful wedded wife have a night out without everyone jumping to conclusions?'

I don't know what he was complaining about. The conclusion might be incorrect but it was a lot more innocent—and complimentary—than the conclusions everyone had jumped to when he was out with a woman who was not his wife.

'There now! You see?' He turned on poor Milly. Suddenly it was all her fault. 'If you don't tell them what you want to hear, they'll throw all this rubbish at you and make us look like a fine pair of fools. Now tell her a proper song to play!'

Only too obviously, Milly went blanker than ever. Her distress was a palpable thing. I could have hurled the champagne glass at Albert Tiverton.

Ted had been standing close enough to hear. He gave his brother-in-law a murderous look and moved forward to his sister's side.

'Oh! All the seats are taken!' A disappointed voice spoke in my ear, providing welcome distraction. 'Do any of them—' Daisy lowered her voice to a conspiratorial husk— 'look like leaving soon?'

'It doesn't matter,' I said, sliding along the piano

bench. 'You can sit here.' It was a favoured seat, although I didn't offer it to just anyone. Only when customers joined me in a piano duet or wanted to sing the lyrics themselves, did I allow them to share the piano bench briefly. But Daisy was different.

'Thank you, dear, that's very nice of you.' Daisy plumped down beside me with evident gratification. She enjoyed an occasional fling in the spotlight again and her voice, although running towards the breathless, was still good—especially in the old Music Hall numbers.

'Come on,' I said, slipping into a familiar melody. 'Take a turn.'

It was not until her voice rose, sweet and clear, that I realized the song I had subconsciously chosen.

> *'She was only a bird*
> *In a gilded cage . . .'*

Our eyes met and I knew we were both thinking of Norma.

'She hasn't come home yet,' Daisy whispered to me, under cover of the chorus in which the customers had joined. 'Neither of them have. It's not like them to be so late. They usually go somewhere nice to cheer themselves up after the nursing home, but they're back before this. I thought they might have come here . . . Well, Norma might—' She broke off to go back to the lyric.

> *'Her beauty was sold*
> *For an old man's gold . . .'*

But Norma was waiting for an old woman to die before any gold could come to her. Or rather, to her husband. And then what? Would she have him declared incompetent, get control of the estate and, possibly, decamp? But the old lady sounded shrewd and mistrusting enough to have forestalled that possibility. Everything was undoubtedly tied up in an irrevocable trust.

'She's a bird in a gilded cage!'

The song rushed to its crescendo, even Milly joining in happily, her recent embarrassment forgotten. She was another fluttering innocent, imprisoned in a cage not particularly gilded.

'My Old Man!' someone called out from the back of the room. Milly nodded enthusiastic agreement, for once not noticing her husband's frown. He would have preferred her to request something no one else had thought of, so that he could demonstrate his authority by insisting that I play it.

'My old man said "Follow the van—
And don't dilly-dally on the way" . . .'

It was a good rousing old favourite. Daisy did the honours with the lyric again while I concentrated on playing honky-tonk.

As usual, once we began warming up, there was a blizzard of request-bearing paper cocktail napkins passed along to me. I tried to stack them in the order in which they arrived so that I could deal with them in turn.

Out of the corner of my eye, I saw Albert Tiverton frown again and then remove the cocktail napkin from beneath Milly's glass. He hunched over it, scrawling a request without consulting his wife. He passed it to me with an air of triumph.

I smiled sweetly at him and placed it at the bottom of the pile without looking at it. His face darkened.

I thumped down on the loud pedal to drown out any remark he might be going to make. He leaned forward belligerently and opened his mouth, but a sudden commotion at the entrance distracted all of us.

'OH NO YOU DON'T!' Ted thundered at someone unseen. 'You're not coming in here!'

We froze. Had the hooligan invasion started? Several of the local men stood up quietly and moved towards the door to back Ted.

'You stay here,' Albert Tiverton instructed his wife. 'I'll take care of this!'

'Be careful, Bert,' she pleaded.

There was a scuffle at the door and Ted bellowed with outrage as a small, slight figure eluded his grasp and darted into the room. The others tensed and waited to do battle with the rest of the invaders while Ted chased after the one who had escaped him.

After several uneasy moments, it became apparent that no others were involved. The culprit playing tag with Ted was the only interloper and he didn't appear to be much of a threat.

The locals went back to their tables; the tourists hadn't even noticed. Although intent, Ted's pursuit was relatively unobtrusive. The intruder slid like a shadow between tables, always avoiding Ted's grasp. Albert Tiverton had sized up the situation and moved swiftly in an opposite direction to corner the quarry in a pincer movement.

The quarry seemed to be leading the chase towards the piano bar. Daisy caught a glimpse of his face before I did.

'It's Johnny Handell!' she said. 'Whatever is he doing here? No wonder Ted is so upset. It just won't do, dear. It won't do, at all.'

Before I could say anything, Little Johnny gained the temporary refuge of the piano, just ahead of the two men closing in on him.

'Where's my mother?' he demanded urgently. 'She isn't home.'

'Neither were you a little while ago,' Daisy said indignantly. 'How am I supposed to know where you all get to?

I haven't seen your mother since you both went out this morning.'

'Isn't she here?' He turned his fierce gaze on me.

'Not tonight,' I said. 'At least,' I qualified, 'not yet. Did she say she was coming here?'

He ignored my question, turning to glare at the customers sitting around the piano. His gaze fell on the one empty place and he stiffened with suspicion. 'Where's my mother?' he demanded again.

'Gotcher, you little bleeder!' Ted pounced, hands descending on Johnny's shoulder in an iron grip. Albert Tiverton approached from the other side and grabbed at the boy's arm.

Johnny instantly began to struggle, kicking out at the men and wriggling like an eel. He caught both men by surprise. What had been a neat, clean capture devolved into an undignified scuffle, endangering the safety of everyone in the vicinity.

Daisy and I abandoned the piano bench hastily as the battle raged around us. The pile of cocktail napkins went flying, the glasses along the piano top shook and several crashed to the floor. Customers snatched up their own drinks protectively, the girls shrieking out in protest.

I moved forward to try to head them away from the piano before they damaged it. I didn't want an out-of-tune piano when interested parties might be coming down from London to watch my act.

Suddenly, with a loud crashing discord, the battle was over. Johnny was spreadeagled across the keyboard, well and truly captured this time.

'Now out you bloody well go!' Ted pulled Johnny upright with another crashing discord and transferred his grip to the nape of Johnny's neck. 'I could lose my licence if you were found in here!'

Johnny muttered about something else Ted could lose for all he cared and Ted visibly restrained himself from hurling the little monster down the stairs. Instead, he slowly and carefully escorted Johnny through the door and we could hear the heavy tread of their feet descending the stairs.

'I'd better go too, dear,' Daisy said. 'Really I had. It's almost closing time, anyway. I'll walk home with Johnny before he gets into any more mischief. He's really upset not to find Norma home. I must say, I don't know where she could be at this hour.'

'Perhaps she's fallen asleep somewhere.' I stooped and began gathering up the scattered cocktail napkins. It would be impossible to get them back into the right order. The best I could do would be to sort through them quickly, play any duplicated requests in their full version and run the others together in a long medley in order to get through them all before Ted called 'Time'.

'Anything's possible, dear,' Daisy sighed. 'Especially with Norma. I do wish she'd decide to leave, you know. The money's nice, but it isn't everything. And she's getting worse and worse. She quite frightens me sometimes.'

'I'm not surprised,' I agreed. 'I—'

'What's the matter, dear. What is it?'

'Nothing,' I said. I crumpled the cocktail napkin in my hand quickly. 'Someone thinks they're funny, that's all.'

'Oh, one of those,' Daisy said wisely. 'Never mind, dear. This weekend will soon be over and they'll all crawl back into the woodwork for another year. Don't let it get you down, dear.'

'I won't,' I said, allowing her to go on thinking that it was either a proposition or an obscenity. I did not want to display the actual message, although it was seared into my mind.

KEEP YOUR MOUTH SHUT OR YOU'RE DEAD!

For further emphasis, it appeared to have been written in blood.

CHAPTER 11

I was later than usual and the house was dark and silent when I returned. I snapped on the front hall light, but nothing happened. I flipped the switch up and down again and was rewarded by a pale flickering glow. The light bulb was going fast.

It was indicative of the state of my nerves that I jumped at the faint sound behind me although I had heard it a thousand times since I'd been here: the soft thud of a cat dropping to the floor from some higher perch.

The faint mewling cry of distress was new. I turned to see Gracie limping into the hallway, favouring her front left paw.

'What's the matter, Gracie?' I started towards her, but she backed away. There was no sign of the other cats.

'Come on,' I coaxed, crouching. 'What's the matter with you tonight? You're usually the friendliest of the lot.'

Gracie circled me warily. There was definitely something wrong with that paw, but she would not come close enough for me to take a look at it.

'All right,' I said, opening my handbag. 'I know what will fetch you.' I brought out the little plastic bag of cheese cubes.

Gracie began edging closer, as though against her better judgement. I shook a couple of cubes into my hand and held it out enticingly. She twitched her whiskers and settled back on her haunches to think about it.

Just then the hall light gave a final flicker and a loud 'pop' and everything went black. That bulb was definitely gone now. I heard the scampering paws as Gracie, already upset and now startled and frightened, darted elsewhere for safety.

There was nothing more I could do tonight. Even if I knew where Daisy kept her spare bulbs, it would need daylight and a stepladder to change the bulb. Nor did I feel up to chasing a frightened cat through a dark house.

I found the stair rail and cautiously began climbing. There was no light on the first-floor landing either. I wondered if all the bulbs had given out at the same time or whether Daisy had had a sudden attack of economy. Or perhaps she had thought that we were all in for the night and had turned off all the lights before going to bed herself.

Moving carefully, I reached my own room without mishap and thankfully turned on my own light. The sudden brightness made me blink.

I found I was still holding the bag of cheese and dropped it on the desk top. The light thump of the bag hitting the desk was immediately echoed by another soft thump as something leaped out of the shadows and landed on the desk.

Again I jumped, and again there was a soft yowl of pain from a cat. But Robey was made of sterner stuff than Gracie, particularly where food was concerned. He limped determinedly over to the bag and began working it open.

'How did you get in here?' I asked. 'The door was shut. Have you been in here all evening?'

Robey drew his head out of the bag, a square of cheese between his teeth and crouched down to eat in comfort. He kept glancing at me out of the corners of his eyes. Like Gracie, he seemed to be in a mistrustful mood.

'What have you two been doing?' I asked. 'Did you get your paws caught in a closing door, or something?'

Robey gave me a suspicious look as I bent over him and backed to the far side of the desk.

'All right,' I said, 'relax.' I bowled another piece of cheese over to him and he caught it neatly, but still looked at me uneasily.

'Where's Formby?' I wondered aloud. 'Is he wounded too?'

Robey finished his cheese, shot me a dark, unhelpful look and jumped down, crying out again as he hit the floor. He limped to the door and stood there waiting for me to open it for him. His whole attitude proclaimed that he didn't have to hang around here listening to stupid questions.

'Have it your way,' I said and crossed to open the door. It was obvious I wasn't going to be allowed to investigate any sore paws tonight. Not that I'd know what to do about any sores I might discover. Daisy was the cat expert and she probably knew all about it and had already started the proper treatment.

I had problems of my own. I closed the door behind Robey, who was gingerly descending the stairs as though advancing into enemy territory, and went back to the desk.

I removed the crumpled cocktail napkin from my bag, smoothed it out and looked again at the sinister message before transferring it to a desk drawer. My first impulse to throw it away had been superseded by an uneasy recognition that—if anything happened to me—it might just possibly be evidence of some sort.

Against whom? Did I seriously think the Starer had decided to warn me against himself? How did he know how much I suspected? Or was he just guessing? Perhaps the expression on my face as I looked at him had told him more than I thought.

Suddenly I was overpoweringly exhausted, much too tired to stay awake a moment longer, fit only to fall into bed. I would think about the problem further in the morning. Yet I had the depressed certainty that I wouldn't really sleep—not the peaceful dreamless sleep I needed to-night . . . this morning . . .

I was right. I dropped off into nightmares, from which I woke at intervals with a deep sense of relief, only to drift away again into even worse nightmares. It was not until I opened my eyes to see a rim of light around the window curtains and realized that it was truly another day that I could relax.

Then I slept properly—and too deeply—awakening with a start to discover that it was nearly noon. I leaped from my bed. At this rate, I'd soon be challenging Norma for the Sleeping Beauty Trophy.

There seemed to be no one in the house when I went downstairs. The cats who, with the usual curiosity of their kind, normally came rushing to find out who was stirring, were nowhere in sight. The kitchen, always a-clatter with pots and pans at this hour as Daisy worked on lunch, was silent.

I walked down the echoing hallway conscious of an eerie feeling of being the last one alive on board the *Mary Celeste*. The chill foreboding of my unremembered nightmares enshrouded me again. Something was wrong somewhere—perhaps everywhere.

Yet the kitchen looked perfectly pleasant and sunny. Outside, gulls wheeled across a bright blue sky, uttering their plaintive cries.

Lunch had been started, although there was no sign of Daisy. A bowl of scrubbed potatoes stood on the draining-board. A half-scraped pile of carrots was beside it. A paring knife lay on top of the carrots, as though dropped hastily when some emergency erupted. The only sound in the whole house seemed to be the ticking of the clock on the outside wall.

My eyes went to the clock automatically, then were drawn by a flurry of movement at one of the windows flanking it. Formby, urgent and indignant, reared up on his hind legs, demanding entrance.

'All right, all right, keep your fur on!' I crossed to the

window and opened it.

Formby literally fell into the kitchen, complaining and purring in the same breath. He jumped from the window-sill to the floor without wincing and headed straight for his food bowl.

'Well, *you're* all right,' I said thoughtfully. Whatever had happened to the other cats, Formby had obviously escaped. Perhaps because he had been out on the prowl all night.

'If only you could talk,' I said.

He looked up and gave a piercing yowl.

'*My* language, I mean.' How many questions might he be able to answer? How many useful bits of information might he vouchsafe? Like the proverbial fly on the wall, the cats moved everywhere. They watched, listened, formed their own opinions and were — alas — dumb.

'Where are the others?' I asked him uselessly. 'The other cats, the other people? What's going on?'

He raised his head and gave me a long, inscrutable look before turning and lowering his head to the saucer of milk beside his food bowl. Now the loudest sound in the room was an untidy slurping noise as he vacuumed up the milk.

'Oh, George!' I shuddered. 'You might at least be discreet about *that*, along with everything else.'

He ignored me, concentrating on lapping up the milk. He had apparently had a long hard night.

As who hadn't? I looked around again, remembering that I hadn't had any breakfast. Not that I wanted much. I crossed to the fridge and poured myself a glass of milk. Formby came over to me and gave me an imploring look. He could get his point over well enough when it was to his convenience. I topped up his saucer before replacing the milk in the fridge.

The slurping noises resumed as I closed the fridge door, competing with the tick of the clock to dominate the silence. I heard nothing else, so it was no wonder I jumped and screamed when I backed into someone standing close behind me.

'You are nervous,' Dandini said. 'The artistic temperament. It claims us all.'

'I didn't know you were there,' I said crossly. 'I didn't hear you come in.'

'Of course you did not. Am I not a magician? Do I not possess the secrets of the Orient?' He had dropped into the voice he used for children's matinees but I was not amused. 'I do not enter rooms in the boring physical way — I materialize in them when I choose!'

His announcement would have been more impressive if he hadn't brought his shopping with him.

'No Daisy?' He began unpacking and stowing away his purchases: the yoghurt and bean curd on his own special shelf in the fridge, the muesli and wheat germ on his own shelf in the cupboard. Even though it was Bank Holiday, the health food store remained open. Dandini wasn't the only customer when the town swarmed with trippers. In holiday mood, few of them objected to paying over the odds in health and speciality stores for items to carry home tonight to tide them over until their own shops were open.

'No anyone,' I said. 'I thought you might know where they'd all gone.'

'I?' He shrugged. 'They do not confide in me. Everyone was at breakfast — ' He hesitated. 'Everyone who is usually there,' he clarified. 'How should I know where they have gone from there?'

'I thought something might have happened,' I said. 'An accident or — or some excitement outside. They might have gone out to look . . .' And not come back? Why?

'Henry Parsons will be at work,' Dandini pointed out. 'The weather is good, it is the last day of the holiday, he will be at his pitch to entertain the children and pass the

hat around as many times as possible today. He has probably taken sandwiches with him and will skip lunch.'

'Of course,' I said. 'I'd forgotten that.'

'Why shouldn't you?' He shrugged. 'You do not have
Punch-and-Judy men in your country. You are not accustomed to performers who do not work regular hours.'

Only another performer could speak of our hours as
'regular', but it was true that, in our way, our times of
employment were as routine as any nine-to-five office
worker's. It was even truer that I was not familiar with the
itinerant buskers and entertainers I had found on the
fringe of the English theatrical world. The concept of
someone with no fixed stage, performing a routine when
and where the pickings looked good—and always with
one eye out for the approach of a policeman—was strange
to me.

Of course, here at the seaside, Henry Parsons didn't
have to keep his eyes peeled for the police but, from what
I had seen, he moved on as often as if he did. Perhaps it
was force of habit, or perhaps he didn't want to lose the
knack in case he ever had to go back to busking for theatre
queues. But Our Henry covered the waterfront. You
never knew where you would run into him and his portable
booth next. On really wet days, he favoured a niche on
the Grand Pier itself; on good days, he could be anywhere
along the sands or promenade.

'But that doesn't explain where Daisy is.' Still following
my train of thought, I spoke aloud.

'Perhaps she remembered some ingredient she needed
for her cooking and popped out to get it?' Dandini was
still prepared to be helpful, but I didn't like the calcu-
lating look that had crept into his eyes. Nor the knowledge
that we were alone in the house.

'Not today,' I said. 'The stores she uses are shut and
she'd do without before she paid the tourist-trap prices in
the ones that are open.'

'You are a clever girl.' He had obviously decided to try a bit of flattery and see if it would get him anywhere. 'You must be a keen judge of human nature.'

'No more so than a magician.' I turned the mirror back to reflect himself. It hardly ever failed. It didn't now.

'It is part of one's stock in trade.' He preened himself. 'Always it is necessary to recognize the components of one's audience: which will be unbelievers, which will be suspicious, which will allow themselves to be enchanted.'

'I hadn't thought about that.' I gave him an admiring look. 'It's not the sort of problem I have to face.'

'Ah, but you do not require your audience to *believe* anything!'

The hell I don't, I thought, fluttering my eyelashes automatically.

'With magic, so much more is required. All those people out there—' He waved a hand at Formby, momentarily transforming him into an audience of upturned human faces. 'They must *want* to suspend the laws of nature, to believe against sense, against science, that the lady has been sawn in half and magicked back into one piece again. To believe that I can make someone float in the air, that I can say the secret words and turn objects into something different—'

Make believe. That was the name of the game for all of us, only magic was even more so. The beginning of it all, the original enchantment.

'Magic answers the deepest human need—' Dandini fixed me with his glittering eyes, half-hypnotizing me with his intensity. 'It calls out to the deepest instinct, the one that wants to believe there is more than we can see or hear, more than the façade we have been taught to take for granted. Things are never the way they seem—'

His extravagant gesture encompassed the kitchen, the half-prepared vegetables, the cat.

'Is time what it seems or is it a thin veil screening us

from another world? Is that the lunch—or the beginning of a witch's cauldron? Is that cat—' his quivering forefinger pointed directly at Formby— 'is that cat her *familiar?*'

Formby gave him an enigmatic look and disappeared under the stove.

I felt a *frisson* myself and didn't blame Formby. Dandini had a good line in patter. A few decent breaks and he wouldn't be on the end of a pier in a second-rate seaside town many more seasons.

'And *you?*' Dandini turned his burning eyes upon me, trying to devour me. 'Are *you* what you seem? Are you a simple singer wasting your precious talent in licensed premises? Or have you come through the time warp, too? Are you one of the sirens against whom men blocked their ears and lashed themselves to the mast?'

Push over, Formby, here I come! But, although chilling, it was insidious. I never could resist a good cue.

'And you?' I asked. 'Are you a stage magician? Or are you the reincarnation of Merlin, come back through the mists of time to search for Arthur and lead us all into the new Golden Age?'

We stared at each other silently for a moment.

'You see?' Once again, his hand described an indescribable arc. 'There *are* more things in heaven and earth than this world dreams of. Who knows?' He moved a step nearer. 'Who can tell—?'

The front door slammed, breaking the spell, for which I was properly thankful.

It had just occurred to me that Dandini's eyes were more than hypnotic—they were reminiscent.

At another time, in another context, he could be one of the Starers himself.

The footsteps hurrying down the hallway brought back sanity and the actual world, without shadows, without ambiguity. Formby came out from under the stove and darted towards the doorway, meowing a relieved welcome.

CHAPTER 12

'*There* you are!' Daisy erupted into the kitchen with the force of a volcanic lava flow. She swooped up Formby in passing and, cuddling him, turned to face us accusingly, quite as though we had been the ones who had gone missing in the middle of the luncheon preparations. 'I don't suppose *you've* seen that little bleeder, have you? Since last night, I mean?'

Although indefinite, the description was familiar. 'Don't tell me Little Johnny is missing?'

'Bed not slept in — and Norma in hysterics when she discovered it!' Daisy said with relish. 'Oh, what a scene! She's missed her calling, dear. Lady Macbeth wasn't in it! She went rushing out to hunt for him and I had to go with her. I was afraid she might do herself an injury, the state she was in. But I lost her half way along the front, so I thought the best thing to do was come home. I don't suppose you have anÿ idea where he could be, dear?'

'I haven't seen him since Ted threw him out of The Phoenix last night,' I said truthfully. 'I thought you were going to walk home with him.'

'He was gone when I got downstairs,' Daisy said. 'I thought I might catch up with him, but I never did. I assumed he'd run home ahead of me and gone up to his room.'

'How strange,' I said. 'No wonder Norma is upset. Where could he be?'

'*Pah!*' Dandini pantomimed a spitting movement between clenched teeth. 'Who can care about such a one as that? The world would be a better place without him!'

'That's all very well for you to say, dear,' Daisy reproved. 'But you aren't his mother — and she *is* fond of him.'

'All appearances to the contrary,' I could not refrain from commenting. Daisy gave me a reproachful look and I added hastily, 'The last I saw of him, he was out looking for Norma—'

'She explained where she was, dear. After they left the nursing home, Johnny wanted to play Space Invaders, but the noise in the amusement arcade always gives Norma a headache, so she said she'd wait for him outside. She sat down in a deck chair on the sands and—'

'And fell asleep,' I finished resignedly.

'Well, yes, she did, dear. It takes an awful lot out of her when she has to go and see her husband, you know—'

'And that rotten little swine went off and left her sleeping on the beach for hours. No wonder he got upset when he found she hadn't got home. He must have been afraid the tide came in and swept her away—and it was all his fault.' I could picture it only too clearly. 'Or else he thought Norma allowed some tripper to pick her up.' That was more likely, with the nasty mind he had.

'They must have just missed each other, dear. If only he'd waited at home a bit longer, she'd have shown up.'

'But he went out looking for her. And now Norma is out looking for him—' I shook my head.

'*And* she has had you out looking for him as well,' Dandini accused Daisy. 'When you should have been here preparing the meal for the rest of us who have to work today. These people are more trouble than they are worth. They disrupt the whole house!'

'I'm afraid I agree.' For once, I felt Dandini had a good case. We were all wasting far too much time thinking about and worrying about a couple of people who would have to fight their way out of their problems themselves. 'Johnny has probably stayed out all night to pay Norma back in what he thinks is her own coin.'

'It wouldn't be the first time he's stayed out all night, that's true,' Daisy sighed. 'But Norma never even noticed before. He was always home before she got up. Now she's found the empty bed and she's frightened. And of course I can't tell her it's nothing new for him. It would only upset her more.'

'I don't see why,' I said. 'If he's done it more than once, then he obviously goes off and stays with a friend. It could only reassure her to know that—'

I broke off. They were both giving me the sort of look I hadn't been on the receiving end of for a long, long time. Years, in fact. It told me I was too young and too dumb to know what was really going on. Both of them knew a lot more than I did—but they weren't about to tell me.

'Such a one does not have friends!' Dandini hissed.

'We don't want to go into that, dear!' Daisy's voice cut like a whiplash. 'Norma would be upset—' she softened her voice, directing her next remark to me— 'because Johnny shouldn't be out at all, the hours he keeps. He's . . . he's still only a child, you know.'

Dandini dipped his head, obscuring his face. He picked up his carrier bag and headed for the door.

'Lunch will be ready in about half an hour.' Daisy was not going to forgive his accusation of dereliction of duty. 'Don't you go far—and mind you're on time. It's chump chops—and I don't want to overcook them.'

That was unusual in itself. Not her desire not to over-cook, but the chops. We usually had stewing steak, pie veal, mutton—things that were cheap and could be simmered slowly in a casserole until the sum was greater than its parts. Chops were an extravagance—but quick.

I felt a pang of foreboding as Daisy lowered Formby to the floor and pulled a bloodstained parcel out of her own shopping-bag. Had she really gone to that extortionate butcher who opened today in order to rook the tourists? She had often opined that, from the prices he charged, he was a direct descendant of the highwaymen who had once roamed this area.

Stand and deliver! Had Daisy really stood still for those prices and delivered the cash demanded? Like a tripper?

It seemed that she had — and was on the defensive about it. She did not meet my eye as she crossed to the sink, unwrapping her parcel. Formby twined around her feet, impeding her progress, inflamed by the scent of blood and yowling his hysteria.

Daisy dropped the meat on the draining-board and fended off Formby's hopeful leap before she realized what was wrong and turned to me with a puzzled frown.

'Where are the others?' she asked.

She meant the cats, not the people.

'I don't know . . .' I hesitated. Should I tell her more? Was it possible she didn't know?

'What's wrong?' She picked up the hesitation. 'What is it?' Her voice sharpened in alarm. 'You're going to have to tell me sooner or later, dear, you know. Was it—? Was it the traffic?'

'No, no! Nothing like that. They're all right. They're around here somewhere. Well, they're mostly all right. I mean, they're not *very* hurt—' I knew I was growing incoherent, but I couldn't think of the right words and, far from calming her, I seemed to be adding to her alarm.

'What is it?' She was almost frightening as she advanced upon me and grabbed me by the shoulders. She'd shake it out of me, if she had to. 'What's happened to them?'

'Something's wrong with their paws.' I blurted it out quickly. 'I don't know what. They wouldn't let me get close enough to see. I discovered it when I got in last night. I thought you must already know—'

She released me so quickly that I staggered, off-balance, and stooped to pick up Formby again.

'Not him,' I said. 'He seems to have escaped whatever it was. Of course, he was out all night.'

'Out all night . . .' Daisy echoed. She met my eyes and we both remembered who else had been missing all night.

Only now it seemed that there might be a more expedient reason than mere pique at his mother. Daisy would murder anyone who had harmed her darlings.

'Come along, dear.' Tight-lipped, Daisy led the way to the basement door. 'They'll be hiding down by the furnace. They always do when they're upset. Let's see what's wrong.'

She went down the stairs ahead of me, still clutching Formby and calling out, cooing, to the other cats. A faint uncertain mew from a dark corner answered her.

'Gracie, darling—' Daisy had no difficulty in identifying it. 'Come to mother. Here—' She turned and thrust Formby into my arms. 'Take care of him while I see what this is all about.'

I held the squirming cat and remained at the foot of the stairs. The injured cats had already demonstrated that they were no longer prepared to trust the lodgers. With the suspicion that was forming in my mind, I could not blame them.

'Here, darling, let mother see—' Daisy had captured Gracie, who nestled in her arms mewling querulously while Daisy gently turned her paws over and inspected them. Hearing the loved and familiar voice, Robey limped from the shadows for his share of comfort.

'Oh!' Daisy's exclamation of outrage sent him scurrying back into the safety of his corner. Gracie flattened her ears and began a plaintive sing-song wail. I had the feeling that she was telling us all about it—if only we could understand her.

'What is it?' I let Formby drop to the floor and approached cautiously. Gracie watched me with wary eyes, but was willing to have me near since she had Daisy to protect her.

'Look!' Daisy was shaking with indignation, she could hardly speak. 'Just look at that!'

There was a sharp cut across the soft sensitive pad of

Gracie's front left paw. It looked deep and painful. I winced in sympathy.

'How dreadful! No wonder she cried out when she jumped to the floor. And—' I looked over my shoulder— 'Robey did, too. Do you suppose the same thing happened to him?'

'We'll see about that. George, George, come here, darling—' Cooing, she coaxed Robey from the shadows, ignoring Formby who twined round her ankles, puzzled at the lack of attention.

She couldn't catch Robey while she still held Gracie, and Gracie had put her claws out and was hanging on for dear life, still spilling out her tale of woe.

'I'll get him.' I swooped and captured Robey, who tried, but was too slow and heavy, to escape in time. Gravely we inspected his paws and found the cruel laceration.

'Why?' Daisy was nearly in tears. 'Oh, I know he's a rotten little beast. He always has been and he always will be, dear. But *why* should he hurt Robey and Fields? What have they ever done to him?'

She didn't really expect an answer but, as I looked at the narrow encrustation of blood across the little pink pad, one came to me.

'If you'll come up to my room,' I said slowly. 'I think I can show you why.'

'You can?' Daisy looked at me incredulously. She had been thinking along the lines of inherent evil. The idea that there might be an actual reason shook her even more.

'Wait a minute,' she said. 'I'm going to lock the cats in down here where they'll be safe.' She spent a few more minutes comforting them, bringing down a bowl of milk, opening a tin of their favourite cat food and explaining at great length that mother was not abandoning them, but leaving them down here for their own good.

There were tears in her eyes when she closed the door

on them. 'I hate leaving them down there alone in the dark,' she said. 'You should have seen them on stage in the old days. They were giants, dear, giants.'

I patted her shoulder and led the way up to my room. I was thankful that I was at the top of the house. Daisy was too breathless from the climb to give full vent to her feelings when I opened the desk drawer and pulled out the cocktail napkin, but her eyes flashed dangerously.

'That's the napkin I found last night,' I told her. 'I didn't want to make an issue of it then. I didn't know who'd slipped it into the pile.'

Daisy concentrated on breathing deeply. She kept her eyes fixed on the rust-brown message. She was beginning to make me nervous. I hoped Little Johnny wouldn't pick this moment to return—his life wouldn't be worth two cents.

'I can see now,' I continued quickly, 'it's a childish thing. The melodramatic wording, the threat . . . and written in blood—'

'And not even his *own* blood!' To Daisy that was the most heinous sin. 'My poor little Gracie and George! How could he *do* such a thing?'

Because Gracie was too trusting and Robey too portly to get away quickly, as Formby had done. But Daisy wanted the psychology explained to her, not the mechanics, and that I was unequipped to do. I had never encountered a budding monster like Little Johnny Handel before, either.

'And what does he mean by it?' Daisy had progressed to studying the actual wording. '*What* does he want you to keep your mouth shut about?'

'I caught him shoplifting in Woolworth's,' I said. 'At least, I couldn't be sure, I didn't actually see him doing it, but he must have thought I did. Anyway, there's not much room for doubt now.'

'No,' Daisy said thoughtfully, 'there isn't.' She straightened up and glared at some point beyond me, in a towering rage. I could only be thankful that I was not the target for such devastating fury.

'He must have been carrying it with him,' I said. 'Robey was in my room when I got home last night. Johnny must have taken one of the cocktail napkins I have around and written the message up here. Then Gracie got out when he left, but Robey was too slow and got shut behind. Then Johnny came down to The Phoenix and created the scene and dropped the napkin at the same time he knocked the pile of requests to the floor, so that I wouldn't see it immediately.'

'That is enough!' Daisy slammed her hand down on the desk top, making me jump. 'That is too much! I have put up with an awful lot, dear. In all conscience, I have. But I've turned a blind eye because I've felt so sorry for Norma and not wanted to add to her troubles. But this has bloody well torn it! I don't care! They leave tonight! Not one more day do they spend under my roof!'

'Can you do that?' I asked tentatively. 'I mean, I thought the law protected—'

'Damn the law!' Daisy snarled. 'There is no law in the world that can force me to keep those people in my house. If I have to pack their bags myself and put them out on the pavement, I'll do it! If I have to set fire to their rooms—'

'All right, all right,' I placated hastily. 'I was only asking.'

'I mean it, dear,' Daisy said solemnly. 'On my life, I mean it. This time, he's gone too far!'

CHAPTER 13

Of course, Daisy cooled down as the day wore on. It would be impossible for anyone to remain at that pitch of fury. She subsided into a simmering rage, but there was no one to vent it on. Neither Norma nor Johnny returned to the house all afternoon.

Daisy spent most of the day in the basement, consoling the cats. Now and again, she emerged to open the front door and stand looking out, watching with grim satisfaction as the increasing stream of traffic surged past at the end of the street. It was a soothing sight: holiday-makers, heading back to London and their home cities, leaving the town to its own inhabitants again.

She did not, I was relieved to see, march into Norma's room and begin packing, as she had threatened. Protocol demanded that she first announce to Norma and Johnny just what she was going to do—and why. Until both of them turned up, the scene was held in abeyance, although I could hear Daisy rehearsing random lines under her breath whenever I was near enough.

Which wasn't often. Everyone in the theatre develops a healthy sense of self-preservation and I noticed that Kate and Dandini were also keeping well out of the way. It was a quiet afternoon, with everyone lying low. We would have continued lying, if anyone had asked us, by uniformly protesting that we were saving our strength for our evening performances. Fortunately, no one asked us.

By the time I was ready to leave for The Phoenix, Daisy had reached that state of controlled edginess usually associated with an understudy watching the leading lady successfully keeping 'flu and laryngitis at bay. She was keyed up, ready and eager, but it looked as though she were going to be cheated out of giving the performance of her life tonight.

'No Norma?' I commiserated on my way through the hall. I wasn't particularly surprised. At last report, Norma had been searching along the front. Since the search had started at an hour far in advance of her normal rising hour, it was possible that her strange neurotic fatigue had overcome her mother-love. She had probably slipped into a cinema, telling herself that she was looking for Johnny in there, and slept the afternoon away.

On the other hand, it was possible that she had caught up with Johnny and he had confessed what he had done to the cats—although perhaps not the real reason for it. In that case, they might both be fugitives now, afraid— quite rightly—to come back and face Daisy's wrath.

'No sign of her, dear,' Daisy said. 'I wish she'd get back soon. I'd like to give her enough notice so that she has a couple of hours to look around for another place. Not that she'll have much trouble—most of the trippers will be leaving this afternoon. There'll be plenty of vacancies.'

'Not if the landladies have ever run into Little Johnny,' I said grimly. 'She'd have an easier time trying to book in with a coiled cobra in her luggage.'

'I was on the bill with a snake-charmer once.' Daisy brightened, reminded of happier days. 'It's not as danger- ous as it looks, dear. The trick is—there are tricks to every trade—to keep them well fed. That's why Zalia always got a dressing-room to herself, even though she wasn't a proper star. No one was ever willing to share with her. It wasn't so much the snakes, dear, it was the feeding times. Mice, you know, live mice.'

'Ugh!' I shuddered, caught between fascination and horror. But Daisy's reminiscences were unfailingly intriguing, evoking a lost world of music halls and variety stages. Had I been born a couple of generations earlier, it was a world which I might have inhabited myself.

'Yes, dear, but even that wasn't the worst of it. We shared the bill with Saldoni, a conjuror who swallowed a white mouse for the finale to his act. Not the same one every night, of course, he had two—'

'Only two?' I asked. 'You mean he . . . got them back . . . after he swallowed them?'

'He regurgitated them, dear. They were specially trained. You can't go around swallowing strange mice, you know. It would make them very nervous and they'd get all jumpy. Stands to reason, when you think about it, that he'd have to have his own trained mice.'

'I've never thought about it before,' I said faintly.

'Well, you do. It takes ages to train them—he used to tell us about it—but without them, you haven't such a good act. It was a wonderful finale, dear. At least three ladies fainted at every performance.' She sighed. 'We had a great show that year and personally I put the blame for what happened on the management. They never should have put Zalia and Saldoni in adjoining dressing-rooms. It was asking for trouble.'

'And they got it?'

'Exactly, dear. One of the snakes got loose one afternoon, slid into the next dressing-room—and helped himself. Zalia found him because he'd gone to sleep halfway down the corridor, but it was too late for the mouse, of course. It wasn't like being swallowed by a human. Well, poor Zalia was frantic. Did I mention that Saldoni had a terrible temper?'

'And an amazing gullet,' I said weakly.

'That, too, dear. He needed it. Anyway, Zalia took one of the white mice she kept to feed the snakes and put it in the cage with the other one. They all look pretty much alike, you know.'

'You see one white mouse, you've seen them all,' I agreed.

'She was leaving the show that night, so all she needed

was a bit of luck. There was a sporting chance Saldoni
wouldn't notice the substitution until she was safely
away.' Daisy sighed again. 'She almost made it.'

'But not quite?'

'Saldoni always arrived late and always in a rush, otherwise he might have realized something was wrong. But he
dashed in, snatched up what he thought was his mouse,
and rushed on stage. Everything went all right—until he
tried to swallow the mouse. Then you never saw such a
performance in your life!

'They had to ring down the curtain. And, of course,
when Saldoni saw Zalia's face—and that snake of hers—he
knew what had happened. It was written all over her, dear.
She wasn't an actress, just a snake-charmer, you know.
Temper! The stagehands had to hold him down or there'd
have been murder committed. And language! There's all
this permissiveness today, but when gentlemen used to
hold it all in, it was quite something to hear when they
really let rip.'

'Did Zalia live to tell the tale?'

'Well, of course, she did, dear. The boys weren't foolish
enough to let go of Saldoni until she was well clear of the
theatre. And her hamper of snakes with her. They took
him round to the pub and poured drinks into him. Not
that he could drink much that night, with his poor
scratched throat.'

I felt my own throat convulsing in sympathy.

'I never saw anything like it, dear, and I thought I
never would again, but—' Daisy's eyes narrowed and I
had the uneasy feeling that she was reviewing the battle in
order to pick up a few pointers for her forthcoming scene
with Norma and Johnny.

'Look,' I excused myself hurriedly. 'I've got to get down
to The Phoenix now or I'll be late. I'll see you later.' With
luck, it would all be over by the time I got back.

'That's right, dear.' Daisy's eyes were turned inward as

she brooded afresh on her grievances—and those of
Robey and Fields. 'I'll see you later . . .'

I headed for The Phoenix, half hoping that I would
run into Norma along the way. If I did, I would suggest
that she stay away from the house until Daisy had gone to
bed. By morning, Daisy might have cooled down enough
to contemplate giving them a second chance—or at least
two weeks' notice to quit.

It was not that I did not have every sympathy with Daisy
and the cats. I did. But I found I still could feel sorry for
poor Norma. It was not her fault that her son had evolved
into a monster . . . was it? Certainly, she could have had
nothing to do with her husband's turning into a vegetable. It
was all in the luck of the draw—and Norma had been
picking up rotten cards all her life.

I didn't see her, of course. I didn't see anyone I knew. A
steady stream of traffic growled along every road,
heading out of town now. Since it was still fairly early,
these were mostly family cars filled with luggage and toys
and children, driven by parents who wanted to reach
home in good time to get the children to bed at a decent
hour. Here . and there, an occasional motor-cycle
threaded through the traffic, a grim reminder of the fears
that had been groundless.

Two policemen stood on the corner where the promenade
joined the main road, watching the mass exodus with grim
faces. I realized not everyone was happy to see the trippers
leave. Another Bank Holiday, another dead girl. Was
there a connection? Perhaps even now, in one of those
cars moving past, the killer was escaping . . . again.

The police could not seal off the town and refuse exit to
the thousands of holiday-makers until they had found the
killer. All they could do was appeal to the public for help.
But the public didn't want to get involved, to forfeit the
last hours of their holiday answering questions, divulging
their names and an address where they could be contacted

for further enquiries. They didn't want to get embroiled in something that was no business of theirs.

Powerless, their suspicion and frustration etched on their faces, the policemen stood on the corner and watched their suspects leaving town.

Of course, the killer might have left town already. He could have taken off as soon as he had killed her; hopped into his car or on to his motor-cycle and disappeared into the night.

Or, more practically, he might have left first thing in the morning. If he were staying at a hotel or lodging-house, there would be no surer way of calling attention to himself than leaving in the middle of the night. On the other hand, if he had booked in for the entire weekend, it would also have aroused suspicion to depart a day early, no matter how good a story he told of sudden illness at home. A landlady is suspicious by nature and as soon as news of the murder had reached her, she would have been down at the police station giving them all the details of her late lodger, just in case.

No, the police were right to keep an eye on the departing tourists. There was always the chance that something suspicious might be noted and lead on to something else. Even as I walked away, one of the constables jotted down the licence number of a car. I wondered what had prompted his action. The occupants of the car, two adults, two children and a dog, looked perfectly innocent to me. Just another family party heading home.

It was later tonight when the police ought to be at their most vigilant. That would be when the unattached, or lightly-attached, departed: the ones without responsibilities to take them back early, those joined in weekend wedlock, the chancers, the singles, the loners, the misfits. The Starer and his tribe.

The front seemed as busy as ever when I reached it. Many were staying on until the last possible moment. Of course, some of them might have chosen a late holiday and this weekend marked the beginning of it and not the end.

It was an unsettling thought. I hoped the Starer had used all his annual holiday time and departed. I never wanted to encounter him again.

And yet there were Starers everywhere. The disappearance of one would not ensure that another would not appear. The one I had spotted might be quite innocent of everything I suspected of him. Then again, he might not . . .

I entered The Phoenix with relief, the flock-papered walls seemed to close around me protectively as I went upstairs. I felt safe here with Ted and the staff to deal with any awkward customers.

I was early, but Ted was already on the job, filling small dishes with peanuts, olives and cubes of cheese. Milly must have been there earlier, for there were fresh quiches ranged along the bar counter waiting to be precut into serving slices.

Ted nodded as I crossed to the piano and began sorting out some sheet music. I nodded back silently. I had learned that he liked a quiet hour to himself before the bar opened for business. I was here, but I wasn't going to intrude on his privacy, my nod told him. I liked a bit of quiet time myself.

It was a formula we had tacitly worked out in the time I had been appearing here. I was surprised when he was the first to break the companionable silence.

'Everything all right?' he asked.

Why shouldn't it be? But there was no point in giving that as an answer. The town was like a giant shimmering spiderweb, with the slightest tug on its outermost filaments setting the whole thing a-quiver. Don't ask who knew what—or how. They did—and that was all there was to it.

'Little Johnny hasn't come back yet.' I answered the

question he intended, but hadn't asked. 'Neither has Norma. Daisy is beginning to get awfully worried.'

'Born to be hanged, that one.' Ted kept his head lowered, concentrating on the little dishes. I knew that he wasn't talking about Daisy, or even Norma.

'No one hangs any more,' I reminded him. 'There isn't any capital punishment now.'

'More's the pity,' he grunted. 'Only thing that would do some people any good.'

That was a moot point if I ever heard one and I didn't bother arguing it. I sat down at the piano and began experimenting with some new—or rather, very old, although new to me—music hall material I had discovered but not had a chance to try out before. Perhaps, now that the season was ending, I could find more time for myself and my own concerns. I could take some time off and explore farther afield. There were all those ferries sailing across the Channel every day to all those fascinating and, to me, romantic foreign ports: Dieppe, Calais, Ostend, Zeebrugge, Dunkirk, Boulogne . . .

I played softly, losing myself in reverie. So many places to go, so many things to see. I had the feeling of a world on my doorstep in a way that wasn't possible in the States. Everything here was so near. A few hours and you could be anywhere in Europe. People in these seaside towns popped across the Channel just to do their shopping in French hypermarkets—and the French came over here for English specialities, and of course everyone picked up their duty-free drinks and cigarettes on board the ferries.

'Never mind, eh?' Ted came over and began setting out the dishes of appetizers around the piano. 'We're all right.'

'I hope so.' Then I realized that it wasn't just a general comment, but referred to something particular. 'What do you mean?'

'Haven't you heard?' He seemed surprised. 'They hit up

north this afternoon. Seventeen arrests, so far. Fighting still going on. Police called in from surrounding regions.' He spoke with relish. If it was happening somewhere else, it couldn't be happening here.

'The motor-cycle gang? How do you know it's the same one? I wouldn't relax just yet. There may be more of them around.'

'I'm not relaxing.' His tone reminded me that the events of last August Bank Holiday were just hearsay so far as I was concerned; he had been an eye-witness and deeply involved. 'But I think we're well on the way to being out of the woods. There are preliminary disturbances, you know, if the gangs are around and bent on trouble. I haven't seen any of those signs this weekend.'

Some people might have considered a dead girl in a boating pool some sort of sign of disturbance. However, I knew what he meant. He was talking about mass rioting and looting, not violence on a one-to-one basis.

'No—' A hint of complacency crept into his voice. 'No, we've had our fair share of motor-cyclists this weekend, but they're the respectable ones, like. I don't think we're in for any more trouble this time.'

I nodded, more to keep him happy than because I agreed with him. A mood of gloom settled over me and I could not keep from thinking about the dead girl. I found my fingers straying over the keys, picking out the melody of the '*Dead March*'.

Ted didn't notice.

CHAPTER 14

After that, it was all I needed to look up from the keyboard later in the evening and lock eyes with the Starer.

The music crashed into discord as my fingers stiffened

and hit the wrong keys in shock.

He almost smiled, well-pleased with the effect he had made, then he disappeared again. Even as I looked round frantically for Ted, he was gone.

A ghost . . . a wisp of fog . . . a curl of smoke . . . *No smoke without fire*. Where was Ted?

For that matter, where was the Starer. *Now you see him, now you don't*. He could still be here. With that nondescript face and — I couldn't even remember what he was wearing. I hadn't looked away from those eyes. They were his only outstanding feature. If he kept his eyelids lowered, he could mingle with the rest of the people in the room and we would never be able to pick him out. Throw him out. He was the Invisible Man in person — or almost-person.

Automatically, I launched into a livelier song, as though the crashing of keys had been a deliberate prelude to a change of mood. The audience weren't paying that much attention. Some gave a murmur of approval at the cheerier mood, but most just continued with their drinking and conversation.

Ted must be cut back. As I let my gaze roam around the room, he was nowhere in sight. Neither was the Starer. Yet the back of my neck crawled in cold and constant apprehension. He was still here somewhere. I knew it.

Just get through tonight, I lectured myself. *Pull yourself together. You can't go to bed and hide your head under the covers just because there are nuts and weirdos in the world.*

Deep down, I remained unconvinced. Huddled into a cave of blankets, unconscious for twelve, twenty-four, thirty-six, forty-eight hours, seemed a consummation devoutly to be wished. *To sleep, perchance to dream* the next few uncomfortable hours or days away seemed the perfect solution.

That must be the way Norma felt.

The realization brought me sitting bolt upright, chilled to the bone, as though a bucket of ice-cold water had just been thrown over me. Shock and pride sent the adrenalin coursing through my veins. I *wouldn't* be like Norma—not in any way, shape or form. I wouldn't give up and turn into a shapeless, spineless amoeba just because the world didn't turn the way I wanted it to turn!

Heads turned towards me questioningly and I realized that my music had become challenging, aggressive. With an effort, I modulated the pitch and tempo of the music. The Starer—the killer?—was somewhere out there within earshot. It was foolhardy—perhaps dangerous—to challenge him. Tonight marked the end of the long weekend; it was time to lie low and keep an even lower profile.

And make sure that Ted escorted me safely to the door tonight.

Momentarily, I wondered what I would find when I got home. Not, I hoped, a pile of suitcases outside on the pavement.

Then I began to wonder where Ted was. If he had been guarding the door, anyone suspicious-looking would not have been allowed entrance. Of course, the Starer probably didn't look inordinately suspicious—unless you caught a glimpse of those eyes. But where was he now? And where was Ted?

Now that I looked around, I noted the growing slackness of the staff, the casualness in the service that suggested the owner wasn't on the premises at all. A table in the corner was signalling for another round of drinks and no one was speeding to fill their order. The barmaid had been lingering beside one customer for far too long. Ted ran a tighter ship than that.

I tried not to be swamped by a wave of panic. The Starer was somewhere in the room—and Ted wasn't. I felt as though my main line of defence was gone.

What if Ted didn't come back before closing time? Would I have to go home alone? Perhaps followed? Perhaps . . . ?

It didn't bear thinking about. Also, there was no point in crossing bridges that might not even exist. If Ted wasn't back, I could call a taxi, that's all. If no taxi was available, I'd simply wait here until one was. If worst came to worst, I could even sleep here. Norma had seemed to find the armchair in the Powder Room comfortable enough.

Wait here . . . ? Sleep here . . . ? With the Starer prowling outside? Those watching, prying eyes would register that I hadn't left the building, that I was still inside . . . alone.

I shuddered myself back into the here and now: the crowded room, the laughing customers, the request napkins being passed up to me. Business as usual, and I must try not to flinch at the requests written in lipstick — especially blood-red lipstick. Not everyone carried pencil or pen with them and certainly no one else would ever write a message in blood.

'*When the Saints Go Marching In*'. I could cope with that. A good rousing number, it ought to get the crowd swinging. They struck me as a trifle subdued tonight, perhaps a bit gloomy at the prospect of going back to work tomorrow.

Or perhaps some of them were thinking about the dead girl discovered in the boating pool yesterday morning. One of themselves, down here for a good time. Happy and laughing one minute, dead the next. Because she had taken up with the wrong person? Or because she had been in the wrong place at the wrong time? By how narrow a margin might it have been themselves?

Or was there some sort of communal sixth sense operating tonight? Perhaps some paranormal emanations given off by the Starer as he moved among them warned the more sensitive that it was best to be quiet, be subdued, lest they attract the wrong sort of attention and find that *they* were perilously close to the wrong person, in the wrong place, at the wrong time.

Against my will, my fingers slowed, dragging across the keyboard in a reduction of tempo that threatened to cast a pall over the room . . . even more of a pall. Perhaps, if Ted were here and the service was operating at its usual brisk speed, the drink flowing, the snack bowls replenished, we might all be more cheerful. It wasn't like him to desert ship at the height of the evening. Had something come up? It was hard to imagine what. In the time I had known him, I had learned that he thought nothing more important than The Phoenix.

So why wasn't he here? And was he coming back? If so, when? Before closing time?

Oh no! I had been watching the door when through it walked the last person in the world I wanted to see—apart from the Starer. I guess that made Councillor Tiverton the second-last person—the one and only time he rose so high in my estimation. All the creeps were out in force tonight.

He looked around, obviously looking for Ted. He didn't find him, but I noticed that the staff abruptly began to shape up. The barmaid straightened, took her elbows off the bar, reached for a glass and began polishing it. A waitress darted forward to the table of gesticulating customers and took their orders.

It reinforced the rumour I had heard that Councillor Tiverton had his financial fingers in The Phoenix pie.

Out of the corner of my eye, I could see that he was bearing down on me. I tried to avoid noticing him until the moment he stood beside me and further pretence was useless.

'Where's Ted, then?' he demanded without preliminaries.

'How should I know?' I could be rude, too, but the

trouble with someone like him was that it went right over his head.

'He ought to be here. What's he doing, buggering off tonight, of all nights?'

'He was here earlier.' Even if Tiverton did have a share in the business, he had no right to criticize Ted like that. Ted worked harder and longer hours than the Councillor ever would. 'He must have just stepped out for a few minutes. He'll be back soon.'

'Will he?' He looked down at me with open disbelief. 'Where's he gone, then?'

I gave him a few bars of the '*Colonel Bogey*' march. I'd been over here long enough to catch on to a few things. There's this great national institution called 'dumb insolence'. After all, I hadn't said a word.

There were gleeful catcalls and whistles as the customers took up the refrain. It just suited the mood of people who had to go back to being wage slaves in the morning.

Councillor Tiverton compressed his lips and gave me the sort of look that translated as: *Don't get funny with me, young woman.* But, with the happy satisfied customers all around, he couldn't say anything. All too obviously, I had struck off their mood and was playing just what they wanted to hear. And that was what I had been hired for in the first place.

'I've other calls to make tonight.' He glanced at his watch. '*When* —' he emphasized the word heavily — 'Ted gets back, tell him I want to see him — fast. Tell him there's trouble down at t'mill. He'll know what I mean.'

Even I knew what he meant. The really gripping question was: which mill? Rumour also said that the not-so-good Councillor had interests in half the business in town, both the going concerns and the projected development, the legitimate and the shady.

At least, it wasn't our own dear gin mill. Before leaving, Councillor Tiverton shot a look around the room, over the heads of the customers, that galvanized the staff into frenetic activity.

'I'll be back,' he told me, loudly enough for the others to hear. 'Just as soon as I can.'

I gave him a final chorus of '*Colonel Bogey*' to march him to the door.

Ted grunted unenthusiastically when I relayed the message from his brother-in-law. It seemed he'd heard that song before.

'There's always trouble at one of Albert's mills,' he grumbled. 'He's like a juggler trying to keep too many balls in the air at the same time. Someday they'll all come crashing down on his head.'

It was a beautiful thought. I wished I could be there to see it.

'He said he'd be back as soon as he could but—' It was growing late and he might only have said it for effect, to keep the staff on their toes in Ted's absence. They wouldn't slope off so flagrantly if they thought Councillor Tiverton was going to return unexpectedly and catch them at it. His displeasure was more to be feared. Ted was too easy-going.

'He'll find me if he wants me,' Ted predicted gloomily. He reached out and touched the dimmer switch. The room darkened momentarily. 'Last orders, please,' he called out. 'Ten minutes to closing, ladies and gentlemen. Last orders, please.'

The clock in The Phoenix, like all pub clocks, was permanently five minutes fast. It was really fifteen minutes to closing, although it often took longer than that to clear everyone out.

I slid into '*Good night, Ladies*', always ready to help a good cause along. Some of the customers took the hint and drank up quickly. The diehards crowded the bar to collect one last drink.

It was obviously going to take '*God Save the Queen*' to get this lot to their feet and start them moving. I'd keep it in reserve until Ted called the final closing.

'I'll see you home,' Ted said, just before he went back to the bar to help the barmaid with the last orders.

'Thanks.' I hadn't had time to tell him about the Starer. I'd started off with Our Albert and that had plunged Ted into enough gloom without depressing him further. Besides, I hadn't felt those eyes on me for some time now. Perhaps the Starer had slipped out earlier, when I wasn't looking—not that I knew who to look for. There was every good chance that he had to get back to London tonight and we had seen the last of him.

And, if he was hanging about outside, so what? Ted was seeing me home. I was safe. The weekend was over. The motor-cycle invasion hadn't materialized. We were all safe.

Famous last words.

CHAPTER 15

The house was ablaze with light when we pulled up outside. Ted grunted, swung in to the kerb and yanked up the hand brake with unusual vehemence. I did not need to be told that he was coming in with me.

Silently he walked round, opened my door and took my arm as we walked up the path. I didn't need my key, the door opened to my touch.

The hall seemed curiously deserted as I paused uncertainly, looking around. Voices, one with a rising note of hysteria, babbled in the living-room.

Daisy appeared in the doorway and I realized what was missing. The cats. It was the first time I had ever entered the hall without one or all of the cats coming in to in-

vestigate. Daisy really meant it when she swore she was
going to keep them in the basement until Little Johnny
was out of the house. From the noise behind her, it sounded
as though the eviction notice had already been served.

'Oh!' Daisy said flatly. 'I thought you were the doctor.'
She turned and went back into the living-room.

Ted and I looked at each other, then followed her.

Norma was semi-reclining on the sofa. Semi, because
she was struggling to get up, but every time she tried
someone pushed her back down again, murmuring sooth-
ingly. Far from soothing Norma, this was, not surprisingly, adding to her mounting hysteria.

'Help me!' Norma called out as she saw us enter.
'You've got to help me. Please!' She struggled to rise
again. 'These people don't understand!'

'These people' turned faces towards us which told us
that they understood all too well.

'Drink some more of your nice tea, dear,' Daisy said.
'The doctor will be along soon. His answering service is
trying to find him now. He'll give you something to help.'

'I don't want the doctor!' Norma's voice rose in a modi-
fied shriek. 'I want my son! I want Johnny!'

So he hadn't come back yet. No wonder Norma was so
upset.

'He's being very naughty, dear, but he ought to be home
soon now.' Daisy's eyes narrowed. 'And then we'll have a
little talk with him.'

'Just be calm—' Kate leaned over to push Norma back
as she struggled forward again. But Norma pushed first
and Kate went flying, collapsing in a heap at the other
end of the sofa.

'Calm!' Norma was on her feet, wringing her hands.
'How can you ask me to be calm when my child is missing?
Look at the time!' She glared around at us accusingly. 'All
your shows are out! It's past midnight and he isn't home.
He didn't come home last night, either. And it's the end

of the holiday! We've got to find him!'

Since the Handels were permanently—or so they thought—in Daisy's house, I didn't see what the end of the holiday had to do with the case. They weren't trippers who had to be somewhere else in the morning.

'You mean he's been missing for twenty-four hours now?' Ted was incredulous. 'That long? And none of you have done anything?'

'We've been looking for him,' Henry Parsons said defensively. 'All day.' I had a sudden vision of him peering anxiously from behind the curtains of his Punch-and-Judy box as he trundled it up and down the front, pausing occasionally to give a performance.

'Anything official, I mean.' Ted brushed aside the defence. 'He's just a lad, after all. It's high time his mother notified the police.'

There was a sudden curious silence in the room. Even Norma was momentarily still and uncertain, head cocked to one side as though listening for something just beyond the far edge of her consciousness.

'Oh no, dear,' Daisy said softly. 'You don't want to do anything hasty like that. It wouldn't be wise.'

'But—' Ted seemed as baffled as I. 'But it's a long time for a young boy to be missing.'

'He may have his reasons, dear,' Daisy said darkly. She gave Norma a sideways look. 'Good reasons.'

And plenty of them. I remembered suddenly that most people disappeared because they wanted to. Little Johnny was a mite too young to be able to carve out a new life for himself, but the impulse must be there. It was not just that the realization of the enormity of what he had done to Daisy's cats might have suddenly swept over him. It was more likely that that had triggered off his basic dissatisfaction over a life lived in a boarding-house with an absentee father, who might as well be dead, and a mother who was practically an absentee, as well. No wonder the kid had run away.

'And perhaps no reason,' Dandini said abruptly. 'There are always those who go missing. Sometimes they return with stories of visits to flying saucers. Sometimes they never return. They have stumbled through the time warp into the fourth dimension—'

He was off again. I stopped listening, but Norma was on the verge of losing all control. She opened her mouth as though to scream—

'That's enough, dear,' Daisy said firmly. 'We haven't paid an admission fee, so don't waste it on us.'

Although directed at Dandini, that snapped both of them out of it. Norma closed her mouth and shuddered. Dandini glowered at Daisy and gave the wave of his hand with which he caused objects to vanish during his stage act. Daisy, however, stood four-square and glared back at him with the look of a landlady who had just discovered a lodger trying to smuggle out the family silver in his suitcase.

'Come on.' Kate took advantage of the hiatus to grasp Norma's elbow and try to urge her back on to the sofa. 'We'll help you. Just lie down and—'

'No!' Norma shook herself free. 'You're *not* helping me! You're *not* my friends! You're just standing around wasting time while Johnny . . . Johnny . . .' She burst into tears.

'All kids run away at some stage of their lives.' I tried my hand at comfort, but tried to be practical, too. 'Have you checked his room to see what's missing? You might get some idea of where he's gone by the things he chose to take with him.'

'Trudi's right, dear.' Daisy led Norma towards the stairs. 'There's no use ringing his grandmother and getting her all upset if he isn't there, nor likely to go there. Let's take a little look-see in his room first.'

In a body, we ascended the stairs behind Norma and Daisy. We might as well. It was quite clear that no one was going to get any rest in this house until we found Little Johnny. I began to suspect that we might soon long for those halcyon days when Norma went to sleep at the drop of a hat and remained unconscious for hours at a stretch.

Norma entered Johnny's room as though she hoped, against all the odds, to find Johnny curled up in his bed asleep. Daisy pushed the door wide to allow room for the rest of us to enter. It was a tacit admission that we might know more about Johnny's clothing and playthings than Norma did.

'Ohhh . . .' Norma looked around the room helplessly, obviously not knowing where to start.

'Start with the wardrobe, dear,' Daisy advised briskly, crossing to one of the hulking oak caverns the English substitute for closets. She opened the door in a no-nonsense way and beckoned Norma to her side. 'Now, can you tell if anything is missing?'

If Norma could, it would be a miracle. She had been in a semi-comatose state for so long it was a wonder that she remembered that she had a son, at all.

'I . . . I don't know . . .' Brenda poked her head inside vaguely. The rest of us looked at each other with exasperation, it was plain that she was going to be worse than useless. The best we could hope for from her was that she wouldn't go off into hysterics again.

'Oh!' Kate had pulled back the coverlet of the bed and lifted the pillow. 'Well, his pyjamas are still here,' she said.

However well-intentioned, it wasn't particularly helpful. Johnny was unlikely to have worried about the niceties of nightwear when packing hurriedly. But her action seemed to release the others from a spell and they moved forward, eager to do their part in the search.

Dandini drifted over to the dresser and began aimlessly pulling out drawers. Henry lifted the lid of an old sea chest that doubled as a toy chest and looked into it blankly.

Kate wandered around the room, peering into the corners as though they might hold a clue to Johnny's whereabouts. Ted remained frowning in the doorway.

'His best suit is still here.' I heard the rattle of coat-hangers as Daisy carried out an expert check in the wardrobe. 'And those cricket flannels he never did wear anyway. I don't know why he bothered to buy them . . .'

'Cricket flannels?' Norma asked vaguely. 'When did he get those?'

'Oh, um . . .' Daisy seemed oddly flustered. 'Just after his birthday, I think, dear. Probably he bought them with the birthday money his grandmother sent him.'

Meanwhile, I had picked up the *Radio-TV Times* lying on top of the television and begun flipping through it absently. What I saw did not reassure me. Johnny had marked in advance the programmes he had intended to watch. The markings extended through today and to-morrow, to the end of the week. If he had been planning to decamp, he obviously had not been planning it for very long. I dropped the magazine hastily, before anyone noticed and asked me any questions about it.

'I don't know—' Norma keened abruptly. 'I don't seem to recognize anything in there. He . . . he must have bought most of his clothes when . . . when I wasn't around.'

There was an awkward silence which made me suspect that I was not the only person in the house who had caught Little Johnny shoplifting.

'He's growing up, dear.' Norma did not seem to notice the false note as Daisy soothed her. 'Naturally he's going to want to choose his own things. Spread his wings, like.'

There was a muffled snort from someone in the room, hastily stifled. When I looked around, all the faces were carefully expressionless.

'I suppose so.' Norma grasped the proffered straw grate-fully, heedless of undercurrents. 'It's hard to realize that he isn't just my . . . my little baby any more.'

I wondered how old Johnny had been the last time he had had Norma's undivided attention. Seven years old? Eight? Perhaps nine or ten? She seemed to have no cognizance of him as an adolescent — a disturbed adolescent. Maybe she was too disturbed herself to admit of possible disturbance in anyone else.

I gradually became aware that my fellow lodgers had thrown themselves into the search with a subdued but feverish zeal. At first I thought they were, in that peculiarly English way, covering their intense embarrassment at Norma's unusual — and belated — display of maternal devotion. Then I began noticing that there was a bit more to it than that. I backed up against the window and watched them dispassionately.

Surely it was excessive for Dandini to burrow down to the bottom of the drawer and lift up the lining paper? And why should Kate, having ascertained that the pyjamas were under the pillow, now be running her hands underneath the mattress? What did Henry Parsons, who had withdrawn to a corner of the room and was casually and in a detached sort of way curling back a corner of the carpet with the tops of his shoe, think he could discover under there?

It was the first time any of them had breached the citadel of Johnny Handel's room and they were taking full advantage of it. What did they hope to find? You couldn't tell me they were just looking to see what clothes he might have taken away with him. Even the cats would laugh at that one.

'Here's his school blazer.' Daisy kept up the pretence, even as she went through every pocket of the blazer. She pulled a crumpled wad of paper from one pocket, smoothed it out absently and looked at it. It appeared to be a shopping list — or perhaps a shoplifting list. She crumpled it again and replaced it in the pocket.

'Here—' Ted crossed over to me and spoke in an undertone. 'What's going on?'

'That's a good question,' I said.

There was no doubt about it, they had all lost sight of their original goal. I decided to volunteer an observation which seemed more pertinent than most of their endeavours.

'His metal detector isn't here,' I said. 'He must have taken that with him.'

'What metal detector?' Norma rounded on me incredulously. 'Johnny doesn't have a metal detector. He wanted one, but—' her voice broke— 'but I told him we couldn't afford it.'

Again there was that curious silence in the room.

'Don't brood about it, dear,' Daisy said. 'He got one anyway. Trudi's right. I've seen it.'

'But . . . how could he?'

'Oh, he was a very enterprising little boy, dear,' Daisy said. 'And there are all sorts of ways to earn extra money. Especially in a town like this—' She broke off abruptly. 'I mean, dear,' she said carefully, 'perhaps he ran errands for people in the nursing homes. They're always wanting bits of shopping done for them and they tip well.'

That wasn't what she had started out to say and everyone in the room knew it—except Norma.

'And—over there!' Norma pointed at the television so suddenly we all jumped. 'That's a video cassette recorder! Where did he get that? We couldn't afford that, either.'

I had the feeling Norma was beginning to catch on. Little Johnny would have had to run an awful lot of errands to earn that kind of hardware—even if the old dears in the nursing homes tipped like drunken sailors.

'Oh, well, dear—' Daisy tried to field the question, but a growing desperation on her face betrayed that her inventive powers were beginning to flag. 'After all—'

The telephone saved her. The sharp imperious summons

rang out through the hallway and up the stairs. We glanced at each other uneasily. It was a late hour for anyone to be calling.

'Johnny!' Norma cried, rushing for the doorway.

'*I'll* get it, dear,' Daisy said firmly. She moved quickly, cutting in front of Norma, reminding us that it was *her* house and her right to answer the telephone. There was also the underlying implication that, if it were bad news, it would be better for someone else to learn it first.

Norma plunged downstairs in her wake and, released from the need for discretion, the others went back to their tasks with renewed vigour. Each was so intent on their own preoccupations that perhaps I was the only one who saw what happened next.

Dandini, with a swift furtive look at the others, pulled an envelope from the drawer he was searching and made it disappear into his own pocket so quickly that, if I had blinked, I would not have seen the transfer.

Suddenly it all crystallized, confirming a suspicion I had had before. The atmosphere, the implications, the insinuations, the desperate searching could all be explained by one nasty word.

Blackmail.

CHAPTER 16

'It's for you, Ted.' Daisy came back into the room, Norma at her heels. 'It's Milly.'

Ted grunted with surprise and went down to the telephone.

I leaned back against the window-sill, mentally examining my theory for flaws. I could not find any. As Daisy had said, Johnny was an enterprising little boy. It stood to reason that he would not stop at mere shoplifting. Not when there was so much more—in actual cash—to be swept up in other ways.

He had searched my room. And no wonder he had subsequently displayed so much hostility towards me. I must have been even more of a disappointment to him than I had thought. There I was, an American with, as everyone knew, all the gold in Fort Knox at my disposal—and he had not discovered anything he could blackmail me over.

However, he seemed to have been doing all right with the others. I watched Kate turn from the bed with a baffled, frustrated expression just as Henry Parsons, who was now operating in a different corner of the room, swooped triumphantly on something that lay at his busy feet.

It was dawning on me that practically everyone had ulterior motives for dissuading Norma from calling in the police. If the police searched Johnny's room—as they inevitably must—who knew what they would find? If Little Johnny really was in any serious trouble somewhere, he was hoist by his own petard.

'It doesn't look too good, Trudi, does it?' Kate had come over to me and was absently fingering the curtain.

'No, it doesn't,' I said, more truthfully than she could guess. 'In fact, to borrow one of your English expressions, it looks bloody awful.'

She sighed and ran her fingers down the curtain. I saw her face change.

'Excuse me,' I said, 'I want to talk to Daisy for a minute.' It seemed more tactful to leave her in peace to retrieve whatever she had just found in the hem of the curtain.

'You see, dear—' Daisy was still maintaining the fiction with Norma. 'There doesn't seem to be anything much missing, so he can't have gone far. He's probably just being naughty—' But as she spoke, Daisy's fingers were probing at the inside of a pair of moccasins she appeared to be examining casually.

Daisy, too? It was hard to believe. Somehow, I just couldn't see Daisy as a blackmail victim. She was trying to protect her lodgers, then, playing for time, giving them a chance to retrieve the incriminating evidence Little Johnny had collected. But surely he couldn't have found anything against Daisy.

On the other hand, she had been running her theatrical digs for a long, long time. Over a great many years, any number of awkward incidents might have occurred. Nothing criminal, perhaps — or at least not these days — but things Daisy might nevertheless prefer not to become general knowledge. Had Johnny discovered some of them?

But Daisy was a wise old bird, it was hard to believe she would leave evidence lying around where it might be found and used against her. All her secrets — guilty or otherwise — were buried deep in her mind, surfacing only in anecdotes of the old days. And it was doubtful that she would have spent much time reminiscing with Little Johnny.

'It's too bad, dear.' Daisy shook her head at me, speaking across Norma. 'If he doesn't come back soon, we *will* have to call in the police.'

By which, I gathered that Daisy had seen her friends repossessing their pilfered belongings and felt that the coast was now clear.

'Oh, not yet!' Norma gasped. 'Not so soon!' She looked around the room frantically. 'He'll be back. He must! Where else could he go?'

Where, indeed? And why wasn't Norma more anxious to call the police? Perhaps she was beginning to fear what they might discover about her precious son. Her gaze lingered fearfully on the video cassette recorder and then moved around the room, as though seeking other expensive items that she had never bought for him.

But there was still an evasive look in her eye. She had not yet brought herself to asking the big question: If she hadn't, then who had?

'You know,' Kate said, 'I think Daisy's right. I don't think we can put it off much longer.' Her attitude was carefree, rather than concerned.

In fact, despite Norma's distress, a pervasive air of cheerfulness was spreading through the room. Henry Parsons was leaning against the wall, hands in his pockets, and seemed to just stop himself from whistling. Dandini was still keeping up a pose of helpfulness, but his fingers were giving too many unnecessary flutters. He looked rather as though he were about to pull a long streamer of flags-of-all-nations from the buttonhole he was fingering. He certainly couldn't think he was going to find any clues as to Johnny's whereabouts there.

'I'm sorry—' Ted came back into the room, startling us all. He must have climbed the stairs very silently. 'I don't like to leave you like this, but I'll have to get back to The Phoenix. Someone's seen a prowler.'

Johnny! It wasn't just my idea. I saw the thought pop into all our heads simultaneously.

'I'll come with you.' Hope flared in Norma's eyes. 'It . . . it might be Johnny. And . . . even if it isn't—' her voice broke again— 'I . . . I want to take another look along the front.'

It wouldn't be much use. Everything was closed now. But none of us wanted to voice any discouragement. Norma was too close to cracking up.

'That's right, dear.' Daisy patted her shoulder. 'And I'll come with you.'

'Oh, what the hell!' Kate said recklessly. 'So will I.'

'Wonderful!' Norma said. 'The more of us there are, the better chance we'll have of finding him—'

Or of catching him when we do find him. If he hadn't come home, he was unlikely to rush into his mother's arms just because she went looking for him. Nor did I like the thought of him prowling around The Phoenix. Little Johnny was a nasty bit of work and he had a grudge against

Ted. I wouldn't put a spot of arson past him.

'All right. Why not?' Henry and Dandini moved forward and we went down the stairs in a body. Ted, looking worried, was in the lead.

At the car door, he stopped. 'I'm not sure I can fit you all in,' he said uneasily. 'Wait a minute—'

Norma had started to run. 'Take the others,' she called back over her shoulder. 'I'll get there faster walking.'

Ted cursed under his breath and chased after her. She was in no condition to go running about the front by herself.

'*We'll* walk down.' Kate linked arms with Dandini and Henry. '*You*—' she nodded to me— 'ride with Daisy and help her try to keep Norma calm.' They started off down the street, pausing momentarily to speak to Ted, who had caught up with Norma and was trying to pull her back to the car. She had begun struggling violently.

'It's going to take more than us to calm Norma,' I said to Daisy. 'Where's that doctor you were expecting? He won't know where to find us, if we're gone when he arrives.'

'His answering service can't reach him,' Daisy said. 'He must have gone away for the weekend and his locum is busy with a real emergency.' She sighed deeply.

'It doesn't really matter, dear. *He* wouldn't be able to calm Norma, either. Not unless he gave her a shot of something and knocked her out. You know what the trouble really is, don't you, dear?' Norma and Ted had nearly reached us; watching them, Daisy spoke in a rapid undertone.

'Norma's not just afraid Johnny's run away.' Her eyes were sad and infinitely knowing. 'Oh no. She's afraid the chicken hawks have got him!'

There was silence in the car, except for Norma's ragged breathing, as we drove through the silent, darkened town and pulled up in front of The Phoenix.

'Wait here while I look around,' Ted said softly. 'Don't move until I get back.' He slipped out of the car, then swung the door back quietly, latching it loosely.

Daisy caught Norma's arm as she tried to follow him. 'I wouldn't, dear,' she advised. 'Really I wouldn't. Just let him go his own way. He knows what he's doing.'

Norma subsided reluctantly and that was where Daisy made her mistake. She let go of Norma's arm. Norma was out of the car in a flash and running. I caught the door as it swung back, keeping it from slamming and alerting Johnny.

'Oh dear,' Daisy sighed. 'No good will come of this. I've always said so, and now, here we are. I wish I'd never let Albert and Milly talk me into having them in the house. It's all very well to feel sorry for people, but sometimes it's a mistake to do anything about it. A bad mistake, dear.'

I could only agree with her. Both Ted and Norma had now disappeared from view. The others — reinforcements, as I was coming to think of them — had not yet reached the front.

'Well . . .' Daisy sighed and heaved herself out of the car. 'I suppose we'd better go after her. Ted will be terribly upset if she rushes up and spoils everything just when he's catching the boy in the act. And Norma might see something that would upset her even more. I don't know, dear, I really don't know. If I had it to do all over again, I'd never let them set foot across the threshold.'

I nodded dumbly. It was fairly certain that Norma would be upset if she saw Little Johnny dabbling in arson, or perhaps he had progressed to burglary. Ted was careless about dropping the night's takings in the Night Safe at the bank every night. I couldn't remember whether he'd bothered to all weekend. Things had been hectic and we'd had a lot more to worry about than money.

I joined Daisy on the pavement and we stood listening

for a moment. Norma must have stopped running; there was no sound of footsteps. Ted would be stalking the intruder as silently as a Redskin through a forest. Now it was our turn to become part of the hunt.

'It will be best if we split up, dear,' Daisy said practically. 'Ted's gone in through the building, so if we go down to the corners and cut up the side streets and then turn into the alley, we can meet at the back door and one of us ought to have collected Norma on the way.'

She moved off without waiting for my agreement. It did seem a sensible plan of action. Norma wouldn't have got far, especially if she had stopped running. One or the other of us was bound to catch up with her. Preferably Daisy.

It was deserted along the front, the overhead lights seemed to have dimmed. The sky was dark and cloudy, the moon sporadically disappearing behind scudding clouds. I looked up, then quickly looked down again. I don't like the night sky over here, it's too unsettling. All the stars are in the wrong places.

The tide was coming in, I could hear the slap of the wavelets against the pilings of the Grand Pier. The wind was rising, bringing a breath of dampness. It seemed that we were going to have that rain everyone had been hoping for—now that the weekend was over and it no longer mattered.

By the time I had reached the corner, I had remembered the Starer. Daisy's idea no longer seemed so bright. I looked back along the front, but she had vanished. She had already turned her corner and I was at mine.

I might as well go forward as back. With Johnny, Ted, Norma and Daisy, the alley ahead was more populated than the front. And Kate, Dandini and Henry Parsons would be along at any moment. I would look foolish if they found me hanging around on the corner, waiting for company like a frightened child.

I turned the corner and walked down the little side-street to the narrow alley. I thought I heard voices ahead of me and, emboldened, I stumbled in. The only light was from the moon.

The alley was something I had only seen from the back window of The Phoenix and I had not taken much interest in it. The Phoenix and every establishment along the front and the street parallel with it, had a small back yard which, with the English passion for privacy, was walled off, fenced off or railed off from each of the neighbouring yards and from the access alley itself. The alley was just the passageway running between the back yards where the dustmen could collect the rubbish and the various deliverymen could make their deliveries without disturbing the holiday-makers.

As I moved along the alley, I was increasingly conscious of those yawning yards behind the flimsy wooden fences or more solid brick walls. Occasionally, there was a gap where some establishment had done away with the wall in order to provide parking space. They were even more unnerving, providing as they did, direct access to sheds or sheltered doorways where anyone might be lurking.

I found I was tiptoeing, not wanting to make any sound that might draw attention to me. The comforting voices I thought I had heard ahead were silent now, not even murmuring.

I had lost track of the distance I had travelled; none of this territory was familiar. I realized, with a faint sense of rising panic, that I could walk right past The Phoenix without knowing it. I had never used the back entrance — not even in the daylight.

Where had everyone gone? I halted and strained my ears, but I could only hear the wind and the incoming tide. Some stealthy silent plague might have wiped every human inhabitant off the face of the earth. Except me.

My heart thudded loudly, my breath rasped even more

loudly, I felt that I was making enough noise for at least a dozen people. And a herd of elephants. I took a step forward, my foot came down on a large loose rock which rolled away taking my balance with it. Involuntarily, I cried out as I fell. My hands caught at the nearest fence — a wooden one.

I managed to stifle my cries as splinters dug into the palms of my hands, but the fence was an old and half-rotten one. It swayed and creaked under my weight. For a moment, I thought it was going to collapse.

Surely all that noise must have attracted some attention. Surely it should have brought Daisy—if no one else—rushing to help me. But nothing happened.

I pulled myself upright and stood there trembling, a new fear supplanting the earlier ones: Was I in the right alley? Had I mistaken the turning in the darkened side-street? Was I now stumbling along some strange alley, wondering where everyone was, while the others were congregated outside the back entrance of The Phoenix wondering where I was?

It seemed only too likely in that nightmarish moment. Anyone who had travelled about in England soon realized that the English were far more interested in—and better at—laying out mazes than laying out towns. Streets changed names half way along, the better to confuse innocent strangers, or they took off on doglegs running miles in the opposite direction to that expected. 'The rolling English drunkard made the rolling English road.' And that went double in spades for mews, squares, places, lanes, rows, gardens, alleys and any and all subsidiary thoroughfares.

I did a few exercises to control my breathing while I tried to think out my next move. Not that there was much doubt about it. A quick backward glance confirmed that I had passed the point of no return. It would be quicker to go forward than to go back.

Cautiously I moved my foot, finding and rolling aside

the treacherous rock. On firm footing, I pushed myself
away from the wooden fence, my palms still smarting,
and tried to move soundlessly.

Was there a muffled sound—a smothered laugh—just
ahead?

'Johnny?' I called softly. 'Johnny, is that you?'

It wasn't Johnny. I realized that with a sudden deadly
clarity. It was something wickedly amused—and evil—just
ahead of me. I drew back instinctively, but uselessly, just
as the new sound floated back to me.

It was whistling. Not the happy carefree whistling I was
accustomed to hearing from my audience, but a nasty insinuating arrogant whistle. It was telling me, defying me,
mocking me.

After a long moment, my brain supplied the words to
that familiar nursery tune:

Oh, dear, what can the matter be?
Oh, dear, what can the matter be?
Oh, dear, what can the matter be?
Johnny's so long at the fair . . .

CHAPTER 17

I stood frozen, trying to determine whether the sound was
advancing towards me or retreating; whether attack was
imminent or only intimidation was intended. I could not
decide. The sound seemed to be all around me. He could
be at the far end of the alley ahead; he could be at my
back.

There are different kinds of terror. Some people are
terrified of snakes or spiders; some of wide-open spaces or
closed-in spaces. People have often said to me, 'I could
never do what you do. Get up in front of all those people

and play the piano and sing. I'd be terrified!' I usually smile and say confidingly, 'I often am.' It's all part of the patter, and sometimes stage fright does resemble terror. At least, I had always thought so until this moment.

This was an icy brain-numbing terror, triggered by the hatred and malevolence behind that vindictive whistle. My worst nightmare had come true. I was alone in the dark with the Starer and all the unspeakable things that were seething around in his disordered mind.

My past life didn't start unreeling behind my eyes, but then, I wasn't drowning. Not yet. Who knew what ultimate fate the Starer had in store for me? My mind dodged that bit of unpleasantness nimbly and darted ahead into a future in which I would not exist — except as an inanimate object.

Presumably the local authorities would know that the US Embassy ought to be notified about the death of a citizen abroad, but what about the rest of it? Would they bury me in England? Would they send my body home to Mother? What would happen to my clothes and the collection of sheet music I had been building? And my piano bar — would Ted send it away, or keep it for someone else to use? And Daisy, left with the job of clearing my room and disposing of my effects. What would Daisy do?

She'd probably name the next cat after me.

The caustic thought snapped me back to life — and a fighting mood. I wasn't going to stand here and wait to be murdered. If I went down, I was going down fighting, but it would be better not to go down at all.

Very slowly and cautiously, I began to move forward again. Every step I could gain was one less step I might have to run, with the Starer in pursuit. With luck, I might make it to a place of safety — perhaps even The Phoenix itself. It must be just ahead somewhere.

Meanwhile, if I couldn't place the Starer from the sound of his whistling, the chances were good that he wouldn't be able to locate me, once I had moved away from the spot where he had last pinpointed me.

I kept edging forward, aware that the whistling had stopped and unable to decide whether that was good or bad. Perhaps he was gathering his energy to spring; perhaps he had tired of the game and disappeared like a wisp of fog once more.

Then suddenly it came again, more faintly, just the last line echoing along the alley in a ghostly reprise:

Johnny's so long at the fair . . .

The whistle faded out on a dying fall. I knew I wouldn't hear it again. The message had been delivered. Or was it a warning? Or just sheer vindictiveness? Someone was playing with me . . . with us.

The agonized scream tore through the night and I knew that I was not the only one who had heard the whistler. Perhaps I was not even his target . . . his victim.

No longer afraid for myself, I ran. Ran towards that terrible screaming and the hubbub that surrounded it. As I drew closer, incoherent words began to emerge.

'Johnny . . . Johnny! . . . Johnny, where are you?' It had to be Norma. She was the only one who would care that much.

'Here, steady on—' More voices became identifiable as I got nearer. That was Ted's. 'Steady on—'

'All right, dear, all right. We heard it.' Daisy might just as well be cooing into the teeth of a hurricane. 'Pay no attention. It's just a nasty joke, dear, that's all it is. A nasty joke . . .'

'Take it easy, Norma!' So Kate was there, too. The reinforcements had arrived. But what good were they doing?

'Johnny . . . Johnny . . .' The demented screaming went on.

And then I screamed myself as steel fingers caught my

arm, tightening in a cruel relentless grip.

'Oh, sorry, sorry.' The hands let go, the voice went babbling on. 'Terribly sorry, Trudi. I didn't know it was you. I thought . . .' Henry Parsons let his voice trail off. We both had a pretty good idea of what he had been thinking.

'It wasn't me,' I said. 'I can't even whistle. Sing, yes—but not whistle.'

'Sorry . . . ' He seemed prepared to go on apologizing endlessly. He made little dabbing motions at my arm, as though to brush off any marks his hands might have made. I had the impression that he was as startled as I was.

'You don't think . . .' He lowered his voice as we walked towards the others. 'You don't think it was Johnny himself whistling, do you? It was so senseless and cruel to upset Norma like that. It was just the sort of thing he might do.'

It was. I hadn't thought of it before, but Henry was right. The random frightening malice of that taunting whistle was just like Johnny. Especially if he knew his mother was within earshot—and that a whistle was essentially unidentifiable.

The thought that I had not been the target relieved me immensely. It also dissipated my irrational fear of the Starer. Of course he could not have been the whistler. He could not have known—or even guessed—that we were out looking for Johnny, so how could he have tried to taunt us with that tune? It had to be someone closer to the situation. And who closer than Little Johnny?

'Where is he?' Norma shrieked. She threw one sharp disinterested look at me, marking only that the person Henry had gone off to capture was of no consequence. She cared for no one except her Little Johnny. It was a pity the concern wasn't mutual. 'Where's Johnny?'

'We'll find him, dear,' Daisy said helplessly. 'Don't worry. You're among friends. We're doing all we can.'

And that wasn't much. There wasn't much anybody could do. One thing though, we wouldn't need to worry about calling the police ourselves. If Norma kept on screaming like that, the neighbours would soon do it for us. Some of the people around here had flats over their shops and already lights were flashing on in previously darkened windows.

'Come inside,' Ted begged desperately. We were disturbing the peace, if not conducting an affray or creating a public nuisance. Not the sort of commotion a publican wants outside of his premises. 'Come along, Norma. We'll all go into The Phoenix and have a drink. It's after hours, but it will be a private party, just a few friends having drinks. The police can't say anything.'

'Party!' He had used the wrong word. Norma turned on him, spitting fire. 'You'd hold a party while Johnny is— is—' She couldn't bring herself to finish the sentence. She looked as thought she might physically attack Ted.

'I didn't mean that kind of a party.' He raised his hands defensively, as though to ward her off. 'I just meant—Look, come inside. We'll talk it over and—'

Farther along the alley, a window was raised and a head popped out, turning angrily in our direction.

'Come on.' Kate placed firm hands on Norma's shoulders, propelling her through the back yard and into The Phoenix. 'It won't do any good to get half the neighbourhood out here with us. It would only complicate matters.'

We crowded into the back entry of The Phoenix behind Kate, cutting off Norma's line of retreat. Kate pushed Norma up the back stairs. She seemed to be encountering less resistance now and I cherished the faint hope that Norma might relapse into her normal state and fall asleep once we got her sitting down. She'd been expending an unaccustomed amount of energy over the past few hours.

No such luck, however. Norma refused to sit down at

all. She paced the floor while Ted went behind the bar and got drinks for us. Dandini drifted over to stand near the door in case Norma made a sudden dash for it. Daisy sank thankfully into a chair; there were darkening circles under her eyes.

I found that I had automatically seated myself at the piano and I pulled my hands back sharply as they began wandering towards the keyboard. This might be the place but it certainly wasn't the time for background music.

Most certainly not for the music still echoing through the back of my mind, music my traitorous fingers might translate into audible sound if I wasn't careful:

Oh, dear, what can the matter be . . . ?

I turned away from the piano to look down on the front. The pier was dark and ghostly, jutting out to meet the advancing mist and disappear into it, giving the impression that it might stretch out endlessly across the water, perhaps reaching into space itself.

'It's beginning to look pretty spooky out there, isn't it?' Kate came over to stand beside me and look down.

'The dark before the dawn,' I murmured, not very hopefully.

'It's a long time till dawn,' Kate said.

'We can't just sit here—' Norma's voice was rising again. 'We've got to get out and find Johnny—' She started for the door. No one else moved, except Dandini who shifted fractionally to block her way.

'You don't care!' Norma whirled back to face us. 'You never liked Johnny! None of you! You don't care what happens to him! You sit there drinking—'

'Oh, give it a rest, dear, do,' Daisy said wearily. 'We'll go out and look for him again. Just let us have a few minutes of peace first. The rest of us need a drink, even if you don't.'

'I don't!' Norma's glare halted Ted in his tracks. He had been heading for her with a large brandy. Now he stopped and took a deep gulp of it himself. 'But the rest of you go right ahead. Have your drinks. Have your rest. It's nothing to you! And you needn't worry about me. I'll be all right. I'll find Johnny myself. *I'm* his mother! *I'm* the only one who cares about him—'

She had us dead to rights. We didn't like Little Johnny and we didn't care what happened to him. We glanced at each other guiltily.

'Oh, come *on!* Let's go and find the little . . . darling.' Kate set down her glass with a thump. 'You win, Norma. We'll go out and scour the whole damned town. We won't rest until we find him! We'll bring him back to you, de—' She broke off abruptly, but it was too late.

Dead or alive. The unfinished sentence hung in the air and every one of us was able to supply the ending. Even Norma. She paled visibly.

'Come on, Trudi!' Kate caught my arm, hauling me to my feet. 'You and I will check the pier. He might—' she threw out an implicit apology to Norma— 'he might be camping out in one of the dressing-rooms. Kids have sneaked into the theatre before this.'

'Here . . .' Ted followed us to the door and handed me a key. 'Go through the Fun Palace. This will let you in. You might take a look as you're going through. He . . . might have got in . . . somehow.'

Our footsteps echoed as we crossed the deserted amusement arcade to the entrance to the pier. It was especially eerie to walk through the place without hearing the electric bleeps and whoops that were usually almost deafening. The dark oblongs of the machines loomed like the sentinel stones of a pre-historic age. (Would, someday, archaeologists unearth an amusement arcade and declare it a late twentieth-century Stonehenge?)

The booths were deep and shadowed, rustling with sounds that might be the wind stirring the plastic curtains partitioning off the backs—or might equally well be the surreptitious movements of late hidden revellers indulging in some secret frolics that would not stand the light of day.

Johnny's so long at the fair . . . But not this particular fair.

Then Kate pushed down on the crash bars of the emergency exit and the door opened out on to the pier itself. I hurried through it after her, breathing deeply of the dank sea mist—almost, but not quite, released from the dark spell that had curled around me as we passed through the arcade.

'I don't like the mist.' Kate shivered as we walked forward into it. 'It makes me feel . . . disembodied, somehow. Almost a ghost myself.'

Like the Starer. The thought came unbidden and unwelcome. I thought I had shaken free of my fear of that insubstantial figure. It was disconcerting to realize that he was still lurking at the back of my mind—if nowhere else.

'I know what you mean,' I said uneasily. 'It seems almost as though we could dissolve into the mist ourselves. If we weren't careful.'

'Perhaps that's what happened to Little Johnny.' Kate gave a not very successful laugh. 'He forgot to look over his shoulder and the fog got him.'

'Dandini favours the Fourth Dimension,' I said. And then, because it was dark and we could not see each other clearly through the mist, and because everything seemed slightly unreal anyway, I asked softly, 'What was he blackmailing Dandini about?'

For a long silent moment, I thought she was going to pretend that she hadn't heard the question, then she sighed softly. 'He had a photograph . . . taken on the promenade . . . photography was his hobby last year. And . . .

and Dandini . . . used to be a pickpocket before he went legit. He used to have times when he got bored . . . wanted to see if he could still do it. So he'd walk along the promenade . . . dip into the pocket of a likely tripper . . . get his wallet . . . then come back the other way and replace the wallet. He always replaced it. Except he had no way of proving it because the tripper never knew it was gone. Little Johnny got a picture of him in the act. Not the sort of publicity photo you'd want featured in the local newspaper.'

'I see.' Very carefully, I left it at that.

'And me . . .' Kate answered the unspoken question. 'When I first came here . . . nerves on edge . . . trying out the show . . . I smoked occasionally. He got hold of one of them. Stupid . . . it could be traced back to me easily. Last year's lover . . . little present of monogrammed filters. Only hand-rolled joints in town with monogrammed filters. It was a laugh at the time . . . not after Johnny got one. Town fathers would be very stuffy about it . . . if they knew. He was clever, he never asked for more than we could spare. And we could always tell him where to go. But . . . it would be such a nuisance, talking our way out of it . . .'

'I see,' I said again. Clever Johnny, indeed, battening on the peccadilloes that could be made to seem more formidable, given the bright beam of publicity. And never asking for more than the traffic would bear, but collecting a tidy sum for nuisance value when it was all added up. 'What about Henry Parsons?' I asked.

'I don't know and I don't want to know!' Kate shrugged irritably. 'I just want to get away from this show and this town and forget about the whole thing. It's so annoying to think a little . . . *twit* like that could disrupt everyone's lives . . .'

The echo of our footsteps changed as we crossed the drawbridge and moved out on to the wooden planks of the pier. I didn't mind it so much here where the planks were neatly aligned. But farther out, there were spaces between them, some nearly an inch wide. I dreaded that stretch of the old pier, but there was no avoiding it, not if we wished to reach the theatre.

Kate wasn't wearing heels, she strode forward confidently. More cautiously, I picked my way along. The fog swirled around us, the sea soughed beneath us. I didn't like this part of the pier, but it was worse in daylight when I could look straight down through the gaps and see the water swirling below.

There were lights along the length of the pier, but the main lights had been extinguished and only tiny pinpoints glowed here and there like the night lights in a child's nursery. The encroaching mist dimmed and blurred them. We kept well to the centre of the long walkway and I instinctively tried to walk lightly in order not to make so much noise. In another minute, I'd be tiptoeing.

Kate felt it, too. Her steps slowed and were quieter. From a sense of duty, we split up as we came to the sheltered benches, each of us taking one side of the shelter. I walked more quickly then and could hear Kate doing the same on the other side. We met at the end with relief and shook our heads.

'Do you really think we'll find Johnny in the theatre?' I asked Kate softly.

'No,' she said. 'Do you?'

'No.' We walked side by side, moving closer as the tentacles of fog reached out to coil around us. Below us, the sea was rising as the tide flooded in. Considering that we were out in the open air, it was curiously claustrophobic.

'I suppose we ought to go round the outside first,' Kate said, as we reached the theatre. 'Make sure all the doors are locked before we go in.'

I nodded silently. This time, by tacit agreement, we did not split up. Together, we began circling the building, Kate trying the exit doors as we passed. They all seemed to be locked. We were at the very end of the pier now, behind the theatre, where the most determined and hopeful anglers fished all day with their rented fishing rods. They weren't allowed to fish at night after the pier had closed.

The sea sounded different out here. For a moment I thought the tide might have turned, but the waves still seemed to be rushing towards the shore. There was another sound . . . fainter . . . almost lost in the endless muted roar of the sea.

'What's that thumping?' Kate heard it, too. 'It must be a piece of driftwood caught under the pier,' she answered herself without conviction.

We moved to the railing and stood looking down into the water—or trying to. The fog was so thick we could not see the water. But there was something down there. It thumped softly, persistently, against one of the pilings, a piece of flotsam trapped by the tide.

Then, briefly, the fog lightened and drifted aside. The small dark form could have been a bundle of rags floating there, but rags wouldn't thump when they hit against a piling.

As we strained our eyes, the form took shape, pale white hands at the ends of outflung arms, a head curiously twisted to one side. Just before the fog closed in again, I saw that the body was tethered to some cross-section underneath the pier by the noose around its neck.

We had found Little Johnny after all.

CHAPTER 18

It was well after dawn before we got to bed. By that time, there didn't seem much point in bothering, but we withdrew to our own rooms as much to get a few hours alone with our thoughts as from any hope of sleep.

Only Norma slept, sedated, for once, into the state that had previously seemed natural to her. I wasn't looking forward to the moment when she woke. None of us were.

Kate and I had quite frankly taken the coward's way out after discovering Johnny Handel's body. We had remained on the pier and used the telephone in the theatre to call the police. They had told us to stay where we were, which was precisely what we had had in mind anyway.

'After all,' Kate had said defensively, 'it isn't as though Norma were a relative of ours—or even a very close friend. Let the police break the news to her—they have lots more experience doing it than we have.'

She was preaching to the converted. I would sooner walk into a tigers' den and try to remove the one-and-only cub from the particularly nasty-looking tigress in the far corner than face Norma and tell her about Johnny. It amounted to much the same thing.

We were too restless to stay in Kate's dressing-room, so we went outside and waited in front of the theatre for the police to arrive. Silently, we had watched the flashing blue light speed along the promenade towards the pier. We were both conscious that Norma and the others were somewhere along the promenade and would know what the police car portended.

The car had just drawn up at the entrance to the pier when, carried clear and ringing over the water, we heard Norma's scream of anguish.

I didn't really sleep and every time I dozed off, the events of the previous hours returned to haunt me. I drifted in and out of consciousness to the echo of distant screaming and the dull metronomic thumping of something soft and inert bumping against pilings in the wash of the tide.

Faces, too, loomed and receded: Norma's, mouth open

in an everlasting scream like someone trapped for eternity in a Francis Bacon canvas. Johnny's, as I had last seen it in life, taut and hostile, defying the world to penetrate his secrets. Even the Cockney girl's, carefree and laughing over her drink, joining in the singing around the piano bar.

Then the sound of water lapping again, and the bodies broke to the surface of my nightmares as they had risen to the surface of the water, rolling over to reveal blueish-white faces. The girl's body in the boating pond, Johnny's body beneath the pier. They floated, twisting with the current, side by side, bumping into each other and seeming to merge until Johnny's body and the girl's became one and the girl was Johnny and Johnny was the girl. And, over it all, the sound of Norma screaming.

The final scream in that sequence was so loud it brought me upright, blinking and groggy, convinced it had been real. It took a few moments of listening to the silent house to persuade myself that the scream had been part of my nightmare. I started to lie back again but changed my mind. I might as well be up and doing as sink back into the kind of dreams that were haunting me this morning.

The cats came to meet me as I descended the stairs. If it weren't for the circumstances, I would have been glad to see them free again. They had no such reservations, however. The concept of protective custody was unknown to them and they had obviously been deeply upset by being shut away from everyone. They were sociable cats, fond of company, and overjoyed to have regained their proper place in the world.

They twined and rollicked around my ankles, throbbing with delight and nearly tripping me as I went down the hall to the kitchen. I could have done without the guard of honour, but I appreciated their feelings.

I pushed open the door, helped myself to coffee from the pot bubbling on the stove, and joined Daisy at the kitchen table. She smiled wanly at me. The circles under her eyes were darker than ever.

'You haven't slept at all, have you?' I accused.

'Plenty of time for that now, dear.' Her face brightened as Fields jumped into her lap and chirruped at her. Formby, not to be outdone, followed suit. Robey looked with disgust at the crowded lap and deliberately walked over and climbed into my lap. From their vantage points, the cats surveyed the table with dissatisfaction. Nothing on it but cups of coffee. They looked hopefully at the cream jug.

'Poor darlings,' Daisy cuddled Gracie and Formby. 'They've been neglected lately. But— ' she brightened even more— 'that's all over. They can have the run of the house again.'

'Nice for them.' I doubted if Norma would be able to find the silver lining so easily.

'Oh, I don't mean to sound heartless, dear.' Daisy was instantly contrite. 'But it *has* been very difficult lately. And now I won't have to give Norma notice, after all. I doubt that she'll want to stay on after this.'

'Don't be too sure of that,' I said. 'Her son may be dead, but that doesn't change the fact that her husband is up in the nursing home. Her mother-in-law will still insist that she stays near and visits him, won't she?'

'Oh dear! I hadn't thought of that.' Daisy went pale. 'I hadn't thought of that awful woman at all. She'll have to know, won't she?'

'It would be hard to keep it from her,' I agreed. 'I imagine it will be in all the newspapers by the evening editions.'

'Oh, poor Norma!' Daisy's eyes filled with tears. 'As though she hasn't enough on her plate. It isn't fair, dear, it isn't fair at all.'

'I don't know,' I said. 'It seems to me that Norma may have brought at least part of this on herself. You can't exactly say she brought Johnny up to the best of her ability. Not unless her ability was zilch to start with.'

'I can't deny she let the boy run wild,' Daisy sighed. 'But what she was like before they came here, I can't say, dear. They moved in three years ago—and I rue the day. It seems to me they went to rack and ruin from the moment they got here. Both of them.'

Daisy slanted an oblique look at me. She seemed to expect some reply I was unqualified to make. I could not decipher what question had been asked behind what had seemed, on the surface, a simple statement of a known fact.

'It's a shame,' I said ambiguously, stroking Robey under the chin. He turned his head and stared up at me. His look was easier to interpret: a chuck under the chin was all very well, thank you, but there were times when a cat preferred a more practical demonstration of affection.

'Sorry, Robey,' I murmured. I removed my cup from the saucer and reached for the cream jug. Across the table, the other cats watched jealously.

Robey blinked his thanks to me and smugly lowered his chin to the saucer. Gracie could stand it no longer. She struggled out of Daisy's lap and marched across the table-top to dip into the saucer from the other side. Daisy's attempts to restrain Formby were only perfunctory; he darted across the table to get his share.

'I *wish* they wouldn't do that.' Daisy glanced at the door guiltily. 'I suppose it's all right, as long as no one sees them.'

'My fault,' I said. If Daisy thought she was kidding any-one, I might as well humour her. But I doubted if I'd ever been the only one to remove a few hairs from the rim of the cream jug before I poured. I suppose it didn't really matter; the cats were clean and Daisy would never allow any cat-hater to lodge with her in the first place. 'I should have put the saucer on the floor.'

'It's all right, dear, I understand.' Daisy forgave me graciously. 'They're dreadful little beggars and they've had *such* a bad time lately. They deserve to be spoiled a bit now.'

Daisy needed a bit of spoiling, too, I thought. She'd been having a pretty rough time herself—and it was going to get even rougher when Norma woke up.

'Well . . .' I drained my coffee and set down the cup. I had already decided to escape while I could. 'I think I'll get a breath of air.' I removed Robey from my lap and placed him on the table with the others. He didn't miss a lick during the operation.

'Don't you want some breakfast, dear?' Daisy offered. 'Or will you have it when you come back?'

'Don't bother about me,' I said. 'Nor for lunch, either. I'll pick up a snack along the front. I'm not really hungry.'

The door of the bathing-hut swung open as I began to fit the key into the lock. I *had* locked the door the last time I used it, I assured myself against an uprush of guilt. Someone else must have been here. I was so accustomed to being the only one who took advantage of Ted's open invitation that I tended to forget that I did not have exclusive rights to the hut.

Really, Ted was far too easy-going. He ought to make sure that people would take care of his property before he let them use it. It was unspeakably careless to go off and leave the door unlocked. I grew indignant on Ted's behalf.

True, there wasn't much worth stealing in the hut, but vandals might have got in and smashed up the place. Perhaps everyone had let down their guard now that the Bank Holiday weekend was over.

I looked around carefully, taking stock. The place was messier than it had been when I last saw it, but there appeared to be no actual damage. The deck chair was stretched out in the centre of the floor, as though it had been too much trouble to refold it properly. The light blanket had been tossed on top of a cardboard box in the corner, all wadded up. Something long and sticklike leaned against the wall behind it. No, nothing had been taken. In fact, things seemed to have added; someone seemed to be using the hut for storage purposes.

It was really none of my business. I pulled the deck chair into the open doorway and stretched out in it, knowing that I would not be able to sleep, but hoping that I might get a bit of rest.

I couldn't. Perhaps it was a mistake to have come down here. It was too close to the Grand Pier and I had too clear a view of it, even lying back in the deck chair. I got up and turned the deck chair to face in the opposite direction — and that was worse. Now I had the feeling that something frightful was creeping up on me behind my back. I could hear the waves slapping against the pilings of the pier and could not shut out the picture of Johnny floating on the tide.

It was better to face the pier and keep my imagination at bay. I got up again, returned the deck chair to its original position and slumped back into it. Now I realized how chilly I was getting. There was quite a brisk wind coming in off the water and the sun had disappeared behind gathering clouds.

Jumpy as a cat. Muttering to myself, like a cat unable to settle, I got up again and went into the hut for the blanket to throw over me.

I shook the blanket out and inspected it carefully — no telling where it had been. It seemed all right. A bit sandy, but that was only to be expected around here. I took it to the door and shook it vigorously to get the sand off, then draped it across the foot of the deck chair.

Something stopped me from getting back in the deck

chair. Something I had seen but not properly registered when I picked up the blanket. I turned slowly and retraced my steps to the far corner of the hut to investigate.

The box was an ordinary cardboard carton, flaps folded down loosely to close it, some meaningless commercial code stencilled on the outside. The box appeared to have been closed in some haste—a corner of flowered material protruded from beneath a flap. There was something strangely familiar about that flowered material.

I opened the box and pulled out a flowered blouse. The feeling of familiarity intensified, triggering off silent alarm bells at the back of my mind. Who had I seen wearing it?

Then I remembered: the ghost-like girl who had stood on the promenade across from The Phoenix on the night of the Cockney girl's murder. Even then, I had recognized something familiar about the blouse, but put it down to the fact that I owned a blouse like it myself.

Now I had the growing suspicion that this *was* my own blouse. I inspected it carefully and the last doubt vanished. It bore an inconspicuous ILGWU label. No one else in this town was likely to own a blouse made by the International Ladies Garment Workers Union. Only exclusively American garments bore that label. For further confirmation, another label said 'Ohrbach's'.

I stared at the blouse incredulously. It had been in my closet when I last saw it. What was it doing here?

And in such a condition? Torn at the neckline, buttons missing, sweat-stained under the arms—and reeking of that sweat and some cheap scent. No wonder I had not recognized it immediately. It looked as though it had been through the wars, as though it had been torn off someone. It had never got into that shape when I was wearing it.

Abruptly I dropped the blouse back into the box and rubbed my hand on my skirt. I felt dirtied—contaminated.

Who could have taken—stolen—my blouse from my closet and used it like that?

I wouldn't find out by turning my back on the problem. I forced myself to pick up the blouse again and put it to one side and go through the rest of the box.

A sleazy slit skirt—not mine—also bearing signs of wear . . . and tear. Grimly, I began checking the rest of the contents of the box. Something that looked like pale yellow bedraggled rats'-nest, but turned into a blonde wig when I shook it out. A wig that, curiously, reminded me of Daisy.

A few pieces of costume jewellery—again, reminiscent. Hadn't I once seen that necklace—looking a great deal smarter—around Kate's neck? . . . Items of chain store cosmetics. A Woolworth's lipstick, still bearing the price sticker . . . It all began to add up to a frightening, unthinkable whole.

I let everything fall back into the cardboard carton and stepped back, as though to dissociate myself from it. But I could not.

My mind, once set in motion, would not stop rushing along that dark, dangerous, forbidden track. Something in me knew more than my conscious mind wanted to admit and was going to face me with it. I managed to block it off for a few final peaceful moments.

Then, incautiously, I raised my eyes. They fixed on that strange stick-like object half-hidden behind the cardboard box.

Against my better judgement, which seemed to have abdicated for the duration, I moved the box. The object stood revealed for what it was. The flat disc hovering just above the floor was unmistakable.

A metal detector. One I had seen before, under different circumstances. Owned by . . . wielded by . . .

Little Johnny!

CHAPTER 19

'I'm sorry dear, dear—' Daisy would not stop apologizing. 'But I *had* to bring her along. I didn't know what else to do with her. I was afraid to leave her alone in the house, and that's the truth of it, dear—'

'It's all right,' I said unconvincingly. It was not all right. Norma sat at the piano bar like the proverbial skeleton at the feast. She did not look as though she had so recently been sedated; she did not look as though she had ever slept at all. She sat staring out at the vista of the Grand Pier, lighting one cigarette from the stub of another. Why should she fear the spectre of cancer? What did she have left to live for?

I found I was playing Ravel's *Pavane for a Dead Princess.* Or did my subconscious interpret it as *Prince?* Perhaps it didn't matter. The operative word was *Dead* . . .

'And that terrible telephone call was the last straw, dear,' Daisy continued airing her own grievances. 'I couldn't believe she'd have the nerve! I said to her, "I'm sorry, Mrs Handel, I just don't have a room to spare." And I don't, dear. I could hardly believe it when she said she'd take Johnny's room! I mean, how unfeeling can one get? I said to her, "Mrs Handel," I said, "that is quite impossible. The police have sealed Johnny's room and I don't know when it will be free again." '

'And they have, dear, and I don't. I asked, but they wouldn't tell me. I don't know what they think they'll find—' a trace of complacency crept into her voice. 'There isn't anything *to* find. I'm sure of that.'

I didn't look at her, I just went on playing softly. She didn't seem to need any encouragement, which was just as well, for I had none to give her. She had not confided in

162

me, none of them had. Everyone in the house knew—or had had a pretty good idea—what was going on with dear Little Johnny. Except Norma, of course. But they had chosen to keep it a secret. Now I had secrets of my own.

I had not gone back to the house after making my discovery. I had crossed over to The Phoenix and called the police from there. They had come and removed the material from the bathing hut and sent in technicians to measure, fingerprint and run all sorts of tests. They had taken a statement from me after hours of polite but firm questioning, which betrayed the fact that they believed Johnny had been killed in the hut while wearing the female clothing and his body then carried to beneath the pier.

I was not surprised that they had gone to the house and sealed Johnny's room. Daisy, who had watched her lodgers remove the incriminating evidence relating directly to themselves, might think there was nothing else to find. I was not so sure. Neither were the police. Little Johnny's activities had been wide-ranging.

'There is *no* way, dear, I'm going to allow another of those Handels into my house.' Daisy's brooding gaze rested on Norma and slid away again. 'As soon as it's decent, after the funeral, I'm going to suggest Norma goes away. Oh, I won't give her notice—I'm not that brutal, dear. But someone needs to talk to her and remind her she still has a life of her own. That husband of hers can live for another forty or fifty years and his mother will never let her get her hands on that money. Johnny was her only chance and now he's gone. She might as well go back to London and get a job.'

I just kept playing softly. Daisy's view of the world was too simplistic for me to cope with.

'I've had enough. Just let me get Norma away—and never again, dear. Not under *my* roof. No more Handels. I swear to you, dear, if I even so much as hear the opening

bars of *The Messiah* or the *Water Music*, I'll switch off
the radio so fast it would make you dizzy!'

Was Daisy really that naive or simply an accomplished
liar? And what of the other people in the house? Had
Johnny really been blackmailing them for the fairly innocent reasons so artlessly admitted by Kate? Had they really
retrieved all the evidence? Or had something been over-
looked? Perhaps something relating to other people? It
was an arresting thought.

Would Johnny have stopped at blackmailing only the
people in this house? He had lived in the town for three
years. What might he have discovered about the shop-
keepers along the front? The people in the nursing home?

And there were all those shady amusement arcades at
the disreputable end of the promenade. It was now obvious
that Johnny had been no stranger to them. No wonder Daisy
had whispered so furtively about chicken hawks. There
wasn't much she didn't know — or guess — about the people
under her roof.

As Daisy had said, Johnny was an enterprising little
boy. No wonder he had had money to squander.

The Phoenix was beginning to fill up. The audience
was mostly locals tonight, shopkeepers who no longer had
to keep open late to catch the holiday trade and wanted
to relax. I wished them luck. Norma's presence was not
going to be conducive to relaxation. I noticed that none
of them wanted to sit near her.

Henry Parsons had been sitting quietly in a corner since
the place had opened. This had not escaped Daisy. She
frowned as Ted brought him yet another whisky.

'Oh dear! I hope *he* isn't starting up again. It's more
than I can stand, dear, really it is.'

I began to realize why Henry hadn't risen any higher in
show business than a Punch-and-Judy exhibition wandering
along the sands.

'I suppose I can't blame him tonight,' Daisy sighed. 'He

wouldn't want to stay in the house alone. It's all too depressing, dear. As soon as ever I can—' she brightened—'I'll have that room redecorated. Painted a nice cheerful colour with pretty wallpaper and new pictures. I'll have Norma's room re-done, too, as soon as she leaves.'

Norma lit another cigarette. I hoped she wasn't going to continue like that. The way she dropped off to sleep, she'd constitute a major fire hazard. I found myself more sympathetic to Daisy's desire to get her out of the house as soon as possible.

Not that Norma showed any signs of sleepiness now. On the contrary, she seemed preternaturally alert. Now that it was too late, Norma was wide awake. Her eyes darted everywhere and she could not sit still. She left her place frequently to walk over to the bar and back. Or to pop into the Powder Room where, to judge from the length of her absence, all she did was run a comb through her hair. Or to walk to the long plate-glass window behind me, where she stood silently gazing out on the pier. That was the most unnerving of all. She was no joy to look at, but I'd rather have her in plain sight than prowling around behind my unguarded back.

The evening wore on and I was not surprised when Kate and Dandini arrived. Now that the main part of the season was over, the Mad Manic Music Hall was down to one performance a night, at 7.30 instead of 6.30 and 8.45, which meant they were over in good time for the performers to enjoy an hour of peaceful relaxation before the pubs closed.

Kate and Dandini headed for the piano bar, but veered away when they saw Norma was sitting there. They joined Harry Parsons at his table. He did not seem pleased to see them, nor did he seem particularly displeased. He nodded to them expressionlessly and went on drinking.

Almost on their heels, Councillor Tiverton entered—once again escorting his wife. She must have come into money recently. Or had great expectations. Even Ted's eyebrows tilted upwards, although he gave an approving nod.

Never one to shirk the limelight, Albert Tiverton steered his wife direct to the piano bar. With his usual inflated ego, he thought I was smiling at him when he sat next to the empty place with the drink in front of it. He discovered the reason for my amusement when Norma reclaimed her seat and he had to sit there with Norma on one side of him and Milly on the other.

Hail, hail, the gang's all here . . .

It was too good to resist, and I didn't. Our Albert gave me a poisonous glare, turned away from Norma and concentrated on Milly.

At least, he tried to. But Milly leaned across him to do the decorous thing to Norma.

'I was so sorry to hear of your . . . your trouble,' she began, in the usual massive English understatement.

Norma looked at her as though she had just crawled out from under a rock and lit another cigarette. It was a moment when I could not entirely blame Norma.

'Here, that's enough of that,' Albert said. 'She doesn't want to be reminded—' He gave Norma an uneasy vote-catching smile. 'She's here to try to forget and enjoy herself a bit, like.'

Even Milly knew that was the wrong thing to say. She sank her elbow into Albert's ribs.

'*Ooomph!*' But he took the reprimand in good grace, for him, and set about trying to retrieve the *faux pas*. 'I mean to say, she's in a state of shock, yet. What with the boy not only dead, but all those things coming out about him— *Ooomph!*'

Norma turned away as though she had not heard a word he'd been saying. Perhaps she hadn't. Her burning eyes moved to scan the room. What was she looking for? Whom did she hope to find?

'Would you like another little drink, dear?' Daisy asked her uneasily. 'It will soon be Last Orders. Something a bit stronger, perhaps? Something to help you sleep, dear.'

Norma looked at her unseeingly, eyes so wide they might have been lidless. She was never again going to escape into sleep so easily, so effortlessly. Sleep was an unknown word to her now. 'No,' she said flatly. After a long moment she added, 'Thank you.'

'Oh, well, suit yourself, dear. I just thought—' Daisy met my eyes over Norma's head and shrugged helplessly.

'I'll find him!' Norma spoke suddenly, vehemently, in answer to some conversation being waged only in her own mind. Her voice was deep and hollow, sounding curiously disembodied, but it carried a deep conviction. 'I'll find the devil who killed my Johnny. And, when I do, *I'll* kill *him* . . . slowly.'

It was a real conversation-stopper. She had leaned over close to my microphone and her words boomed out through the room. I was so startled, I forgot what I was playing and lifted my hands from the keyboard. The sudden silence emphasized her vow.

After a moment someone gave a nervous laugh and conversation resumed. I dropped my hands back to the keyboard. I couldn't remember what I had been rendering. It didn't matter . . . play something quickly . . . anything . . .

I'll see you again . . .

No, no, that wasn't right. Fuel to the flames. I broke off abruptly, my mind a blank. Something else . . . what?

'Yes.' Norma turned her burning eyes on me. '*You* know. You understand . . .'

'No,' I denied quickly. 'I'm sorry. It was a mistake. I—

I'm sorry . . .' My hands fell to the keyboard again, vamping a bridge. But a bridge to what melody? Every tune that sprang to mind seemed suddenly fraught with *double entendre*. I dared not let my fingers rove at will among the keys—they had already proved too untrustworthy.

'Come along, dear,' Daisy said practically. 'It's time we were getting home. They'll be closing here, anyway, any minute.'

'Not for another half-hour.' It was clear that Norma wasn't going to budge. She turned again and scanned the room, leaving a ripple of shudders in the wake of her gaze.

'Have it your way, dear.' Daisy shrugged and seemed to surrender. Perhaps I was the only one to notice the quick sweep of her hand. Her drink went flying into Norma's lap.

'Oh! Oh! I'm so sorry, dear! How clumsy of me!' Daisy caught up some of my pile of paper napkins and dabbed ineffectually at the pool of gin and tonic.

Norma leaped to her feet, the glass hit the floor and rolled away from her. She shook her skirt and brushed at it.

'Come along, dear.' Daisy took her arm. 'We'll go to the Powder Room and get you tidied up—'

Unresisting for a change, Norma allowed herself to be led away. Daisy looked back at me with a meaningful nod. Obviously, she was going to whisk Norma straight home as soon as she was dried off.

'Whew!' Councillor Tiverton pulled a handkerchief from his pocket and mopped at his brow. 'That was tricky! Getting real nasty, that was. Someone's going to have to do something about that woman. She's going straight off the rails—'

'Some people might think she had good reason.' I tried to keep my voice steady, tried to look and sound normal. Above all, I tried not to let him see that I had noticed the

tiny object that had dropped from his handkerchief and
skittered across the piano top. He must not guess that I
recognized it and that it conveyed any meaning to me.

It was a flower-shaped button. One of the buttons from
my blouse. The blouse Johnny Handel had stolen and worn.

The blouse he had been wearing when he met his killer.

CHAPTER 20

Under the guise of sorting through the request numbers
on the cocktail napkins Daisy hadn't used in her mopping-
up process, I managed to drop a couple of napkins over
the button. I could retrieve it later, it wouldn't be wise to
try right now under Albert Tiverton's watchful eyes.

I looked around for Ted, but he was gone. The police
were never around when you needed them, either. I bit
down on a slightly hysterical giggle. That was something
else that wouldn't be wise.

There was a more-or-less-private public telephone in
the back hall, at the top of the stairs. I could call the
police from there. All I had to do was get to it.

Carefully arranging a smile on my face, I slid off the
piano bench. 'Just taking five,' I said airily, to no one in
particular, and walked off without looking back.

I threaded my way through the tables, ignoring Kate's
wave of invitation. For as long as possible, I headed in the
direction of the Powder Room, in case I was being watched.
At the last moment, I changed direction and slipped
through the emergency exit to the back hall.

The pay-phone hanging on the wall shone like a
beacon. It was not in use. I lifted the receiver and heard
the comforting purr of the dial tone. I had a five-pence
piece clutched in my hand and I balanced it in the slot,
ready to ram it home when the police answered at the

other end of the line. I began to dial the number I had unconsciously memorized earlier in the day.

'Now then, you don't want to do that!' A hand slammed down on the hook, cutting me off. 'Now, why don't we go downstairs and—?'

I eluded his descending hand and rushed back through the emergency exit into the saloon bar. I knew I wouldn't be able to make it in a straight dash back to the piano. The thing to do was to appear calm and unhurried. I had to act as though everything was normal and the worst I suspected of the Councillor was that he was making yet another boring pass.

A small nondescript little man sat alone at the table just inside the door. I had not noticed him on my way out — he was not the noticeable type. Never mind, any port in a storm. I stopped at his table and pulled out the chair facing him.

'The line was busy,' I said chattily. 'I'll just sit here, if you don't mind, and try again in a minute—'

He raised his head and those pale smoky eyes transfixed me. The Starer.

I stood frozen, unable to move or even to continue speaking. He was no port — and the storm was all around me. I was truly caught between the devil and the deep blue sea.

'That's right.' Hands like iron bands grappled me from behind and pulled me backwards. 'We'll try again.' I was pushed through the emergency exit before I could catch my breath to scream.

At the top of the stairs, he changed his grip. One hand clamped across my mouth, too quickly for me to bite. Twisting my arm behind my back, he propelled me down the stairs at top speed. I caught at the stair rail with my free hand to keep from falling. He would not care if I hurtled headlong and broke my neck. It would save him the bother of breaking it himself later.

He had to let go of my arm to open the back door. Before I could catch my balance, he had reclaimed the arm and bundled me out of the door and into the back yard.

The door swung shut behind us and we both hesitated at the sudden darkness. Then he began pushing me forward again, he was more familiar with the area than I was and, presumably, he had some destination in mind.

I dug in my heels and resisted. He was not going to get me out into the alley without a fight — preferably a noisy one. Once we were out of the backyard, he might go any-where. No one would be able to find us. If they came looking, that is.

With a muttered curse, he brought his knee up into the back of my knees and they buckled under me. He held me upright as I sagged and kept moving forward inexorably. We were at the gate now, another moment and we would be out in the alley and I would be lost.

He cursed again as he realized the gate opened inward and he would have to free one hand to open it. I could feel his mental turmoil as he tried to decide whether to uncover my mouth or free my arm.

He opted for the arm, ramming me against the gatepost with his hip to hold me immobilized. If he got me through that gate, I was as good as done for. It was agonizing to think that just behind me and up one flight of stairs friends were laughing and talking, unaware of my peril. Surely someone must soon notice that I had been gone longer than usual and begin to wonder.

Daisy must soon shepherd Norma out of the Powder Room and start for home. Would she glance towards the vacant piano bench and wonder where I'd gone? Ted must be back by now. Wouldn't he be surprised — and per-haps indignant — not to find me there playing the 'drinking-up music' as he called out for last orders? Wasn't Milly getting jealous as she realized that the pianist and her

precious husband were both missing? Had Kate and the
others noticed that I had gone through the back door
with the man I most despised? That must have occasioned
some surprise—especially as I hadn't returned. What did
they imagine we were doing? Even if they thought we were
burying the hatchet, they must think we were taking an
unconscionable time about it.

But perhaps no one had noticed anything at all. I had
probably not been gone all that long. Even though my life-
expectancy had telescoped down to its last few moments,
in terms of actual time consumed, the whole process had
not taken more than three or four minutes.

Albert Tiverton uttered a wordless snarl as he discovered
the gate was locked. He suddenly hurled me from him,
slamming me against the fence and pinioning me there by
the throat with one hand as he fumbled for something in
his pocket.

My throat was dry and my lips numb from being ground
against my teeth, but I could speak again. Not too loudly.
That hand around my throat had only to press a bit harder
to crush my windpipe. I wanted to begin a dialogue, not
startle him into killing me instantly.

'Ted locked it last night,' I whispered. 'There was a
prowler—' Realization struck me belatedly. He knew all
about it. 'It was you!'

'Just doing my rounds. He spoke with suppressed fury.
'Some fool saw me but didn't recognize me. Tried to telephone Ted, but couldn't reach him. Telephoned my
home, knowing I was part-owner of this place. Milly took
the call. I wasn't home, so she managed to find Ted and
send him off on the wild goose chase—'

He found what he wanted and pulled a large bunch of
keys from his pocket. Enough keys for half the premises in
town. I began to realize what he meant when he spoke of
doing his rounds. He must have a key to every place in
which he owned a financial interest. He would have access to

most of the buildings along the front . . . And the boating
pool?

'It was you . . . that terrible mocking whistle. You
killed Little Johnny. But why . . . ?' It was an unnecessary
question. I was in a situation that concentrated the mind
wonderfully. I caught the distant whiff of civic corruption.
Little Johnny had gone everywhere along the front, prying
and spying. 'I suppose he knew too much?'

'That, too.' He was trying to sort out the keys one-handed
to find the right one for the gate. 'More reasons than one,
the little bastard had it coming to him.'

'How could you?' I choked. 'He was just a little boy—'

'Oh no.' He gave a grim laugh. 'No, he wasn't. I don't
know what he was, but a boy he was not. Little—' He
broke off tried to fit one of the keys into the lock.

'Just the same—' I tried to distract him, to keep him
from realizing that some strength was returning to my
aching arm— 'it was unnecessary. No one would have
taken his word against yours—' No, but it might have
started them wondering. There was more to it than that,
though. The torn clothing, the taunting whistle, bespoke
a more personal malice. 'What had he ever done to you?'

'Done? Done?' I shrank back from his explosive fury.
'I'll tell you what he done! Luring me on! With his painted
face and his female clothes. I didn't recognize him. How
could I? Who'd have expected—?'

'Even so . . .' I said.

'I'd had a hard day.' He was momentarily plaintive, the
need to justify himself was strong. 'A man's entitled to
some fun. I took Milly home and came back to the front
that night. Middle of a holiday weekend, lots of trippers
around, girls looking for a good time on a Saturday
night . . .'

Saturday night . . . my mind filled in the gaps. That
was the night Norma had escaped him . . . and his wife
had caught up with him. He must have been seething

with frustration.

It was also the night a pretty little ghost-girl had been loitering alone across the street from The Phoenix. Johnny . . . keeping a jealous eye on his mother? Or looking for a pick-up? Or perhaps a bit of both.

'So I came back to the front and met up with this *girl* — this *tripper* —' He was swept along on a tide of righteous indignation, but it didn't stop him from trying another key in the lock. Any moment, he was bound to find the right one.

'How was I to know? How could any normal man expect—? He led me on, then he began to laugh at me. He thought I *did* know—or pretended he thought so. Then he broke away and ran—still laughing. I chased him—what else could I do? He ran down the dark alleys—he knew them all. He would. I followed the laughing until it stopped. And then I heard it behind me and I thought he'd doubled back. I swung around and caught him— her—by the throat. I'd teach the little sod to laugh at me!'

His hand tightened convulsively on my own throat. My blood thrummed in my ears, rays of light exploded behind my eyes. I clawed at his hand desperately, but he didn't seem to notice. He was reliving the recent past. It had happened then, too.

'He stopped laughing, all right. I held on to him for a minute longer, to teach him a lesson, like. Then I gave him a good shaking and dragged him under the street light to frighten him some more. But when I looked down, it wasn't him—it was her. And she was dead—' His voice hardened. 'But she'd laughed at me, too. She'd seen what happened with Johnny and she thought it was funny. She'd laughed earlier, too, around the piano—'

The girl in the boating pond. His hand was too tight for me to speak. He had found the right key and was fitting it in the lock absently, his mind still going over the scene he had been describing. He'd have the key to the boating pond gate, too. Would he risk dumping another body there?

'He got away—that time. But he'd watched what had happened to the girl. After the police discovered the body, he rang me, wanted money. He was a fly one, but he still had to arrange to collect the money—'

Oh, Johnny, Johnny, I thought sadly. *If only you hadn't been so greedy . . .*

'He had the gall to wear that outfit again—' Tiverton's voice choked with righteous indignation. 'To come mincing along like—like a woman of the streets! He looked around, but he didn't see me where I'd hidden myself. I watched him pick up the parcel and I followed him back to the bathing-hut where he'd been hiding out. And I—' He broke off, turned the key in the lock, and pulled the gate inward.

'You killed him there,' I managed to whisper.

'Aye—and I stripped the deceiving finery off him before I strung him up under the pier. Born to be hanged, that one was, and he made it. I washed his face off, too, before I left him. It was the least I could do for poor Norma.'

'You're all heart.' I no longer cared whether I antagonized him. I braced myself for the final struggle.

'And now you—' He wasn't going to waste any more time. Still holding me with one hand, he drew back his other hand to knock me unconscious. I tried to scream, but all that came out was a whimper of alarm. I closed my eyes against the blow.

There was a crunching noise. He gave a strange grunt and then I heard a thud.

I opened my eyes to find him in a heap at my feet. Half of a heavy glass ashtray lay beside his head.

I looked up and straight into the eyes of the Starer. I found my voice then and began screaming.

The light over the back door went on abruptly, floodlighting the back yard. The back door burst open—it had already been opened once. I realized that was the source of the light rays I had thought were due to my having been half-strangled.

Then they were all around me. Kate and Dandini supporting me, Daisy holding Norma back. Ted stood looking down at his brother-in-law with horrified resignation.

'Are you all right, Miss Kane?' the Starer asked earnestly. 'I heard everything he said. It was awful. I hope you don't mind that I had to resort to violence—' He was still clutching the other half of the glass ashtray. 'But he was going to hit you and I couldn't let him do that. So I hit him first with the ashtray. I—I'm sorry. I know it wasn't cricket, but he's bigger than I am—'

Upstairs, after the police had come and gone, he was still contrite. 'I'm sorry I broke the ashtray—' He looked around to apologize to Ted, but Ted had taken a dazed Milly and Norma to a nursing home and wasn't back yet. We were down to a private party again, a few friends drinking after hours.

'It was such heavy glass,' he said. 'I didn't think it would break so easily—'

'Never mind the ashtray! I'll buy you another.' I threw my arms around him wildly and kissed him. I'd been doing rather a lot of that in the past couple of hours. To everybody. It was so good to be alive. 'I'll buy you a dozen ashtrays!'

'Oh no, thank you,' he said primly. 'I don't smoke.'

'That Albert Tiverton always did have a head that could break a cement block,' Daisy said.

Sidney, ex-the Starer, turned his large eyes towards me. They were really rather attractive eyes, now that they were focused properly. There was nothing to fear from him. There might be, probably would be, other Starers, and one of them might be deadly one day. It was the fear every performer had to learn to live with, especially in these times. But Sidney was all right.

'Actually,' he said, 'I've been following you about for days. I hope you don't mind, Miss Kane—'

'Trudi, please.'

'Trudi—' He blushed. 'I've been trying to get up the nerve to speak to you. I saw you in the music store buying some old sheet music, so I knew our interests were similar. Then I found you were appearing here and I came every chance I could get—'

Thereby nearly reducing me to a nervous wreck. But I couldn't say that. I must never admit it. He'd be horrified.

Meanwhile, I was beginning to get a bit nervous about the way the conversation was going. I hoped he wasn't about to make a Declaration. I was grateful to him for saving my life, but I didn't feel like consigning the rest of that life to his care for evermore.

'It was so marvellous when you came to sit at my table tonight,' he went on. 'It was like the answer to a prayer— and I knew I could talk to you then. But that man came up and took you away. I didn't have the feeling that you wanted to go—'

'You were *so* right, Sidney,' I murmured.

'I thought it over for a bit—I'm sorry I took so long. And then I followed you. I don't know why I took the ash-tray with me. I—I guess I felt something might be wrong—'

'Well, thank heavens you did,' Daisy said warmly. 'Let me get you another drink.'

'No, thank you,' he said. 'I don't drink much. What I'd really like . . .' He hesitated.

'Go on,' I said cautiously.

'What I'd like— I mean, I wouldn't bother you *every* night . . . perhaps not even every week . . but once in a while . . . if you'd be so kind . . .'

They were all watching him with fascination. He became conscious of this and blushed.

'You see,' he explained earnestly, 'my mother doesn't approve. She says I'm driving her crazy. The neighbours don't like it either. And I thought perhaps you wouldn't mind—'

'Go on,' I said again . . . This had begun to sound familiar. Only the accent was different.

'I'm not bad. I assure you, I'm not. And I wouldn't get in your way . . . drown you out. Just softly . . . in the background . . .'

'Drums,' I said. 'You play the drums.'

'That's right.' He beamed at me. We had achieved a meeting of minds. 'I've got my own set. I thought I could leave them here. And . . . and perhaps we could even work out some arrangements together. Oh, not if it's too much bother—' He was apologetic again. 'I just thought—'

'It's a lovely thought, Sidney,' I said. The price could have been a lot higher. 'You've got yourself a deal.'